To Sophia —
    Make the most
of every opportunity!
    Ephesians 5:15-17

    ☺ Rebekah Joy

Also by Rebekah Joy:

7:21 – A Gripping Account of Religious Deception and Divine Pursuit

Adventures with Purity

The Real-Life Escapades of a Curious & Courageous Teenage Girl

Rebekah Joy

WestBow
PRESS
A DIVISION OF THOMAS NELSON

Scripture quotations are taken from the Holy Bible, New Living
Translation, copyright © 1996, 2004, 2007 by Tyndale House
Foundation. Used by permission of Tyndale House Publishers,
Inc., Carol Stream, Illinois 60188. All rights reserved.

WestBow Press books may be ordered through booksellers or by contacting:

WestBow Press
A Division of Thomas Nelson
1663 Liberty Drive
Bloomington, IN 47403
www.westbowpress.com
1-(866) 928-1240

ISBN: 978-1-4497-9355-5 (sc)
ISBN: 978-1-4497-9356-2 (e)

Library of Congress Control Number: 2013907746

Printed in the United States of America.

WestBow Press rev. date: 04/30/2013

To some incredibly special young women:

♥ Micaiah Joy—your compassionate heart and love of laughter bring encouragement and joy to those in your life! God speaks to you, and you are wise to pay attention to the messages He is communicating. He has given you the grace to love others deeply. No matter what happens, choosing to love with God's love is always worth it.

♥ Eden Grace—your enthusiasm for life is contagious, and your hugs and giggles are priceless! You bring a smile to the face of all who encounter you. God has given you courage, as well as spiritual eyes that see His kingdom with trusting faith and certainty. Others will better understand His true nature as they see Him through your eyes.

♥ Kiersten—your kind heart and sweet countenance are refreshing! Through His Spirit, God has equipped you with everything you will ever need to live victoriously and abundantly. Jesus is your friend that sticks closer than a brother; you can always count on Him. You are God's treasured daughter—He loves you unconditionally!

♥ Angelina—you have been uniquely called out by God and divinely positioned for a remarkable destiny. A natural leader, you are also patient, loyal, and kind. Always remember how much your heavenly Father loves you, and may His love empower you to speak the truth boldly and without compromise.

Contents

Author's Note

Our society places enormous value on titles, positions, and external successes. Far-too-often we are programmed to believe that "heroes" or "idols" are individuals with exceptional athletic or musical ability, flawless outward appearances, charismatic personalities, elite financial status, or some other achievement that results in fame and recognition.

But are those superficial qualities really what define a hero? Or perhaps are there deeper character traits that better depict who should be revered and followed? This description won't likely ever be found in *Cosmopolitan* or *GQ* magazines, but I believe the ones most worthy of our admiration and respect are those who faithfully reflect the heart of Jesus ... those who embrace the mantle of humility, give of themselves, and proclaim truth—often without a large audience to publicly applaud their actions.

I've been blessed to know and love some incredible women who are genuine heroes. All of them have in some way been entrusted with influencing younger women. Some became mothers biologically, while others entered into motherhood through marriage. Some have tapped into the heart of God and received children through the powerful avenue of adoption. Still others are spiritual mothers who breathe life into the hearts and spirits of daughters who need their nurturing touch.

Without exception, they love unconditionally, give sacrificially, and extend much mercy and grace—while also heeding timeless Biblical wisdom to train with discipline when necessary. Some have walked the indescribably painful road of saying good-bye to a child through physical separation or emotional abandonment. Others have faced the additional challenges of single parenting, working outside the home, battling health issues, or caring for aging parents.

The following women are *life-givers* who are worthy of much admiration for the many ways in which they represent the life-giving aspect of God's nature. They are also warriors who have joined the battle against a culture that aggressively pursues and seeks to capture the hearts and minds of young women. It is a great honor to have these heroes endorse *Adventures with Purity*. I ask God to abundantly bless each one and to continually fill them with His love … giving them the wisdom of Jesus and the counsel of His Spirit as they pour into the precious young women who have been entrusted to their care.

—Rebekah Joy, May 2013

Recommendations for Adventures with Purity

"*Adventures with Purity* is refreshing, honest, and unique! Purity's journey is relevant not only to my daughters' lives, but to mine as well. As I read, I found myself reliving many of my tween and teen experiences, and receiving deeper levels of healing for issues that easily get swept under the rug and dismissed as 'the past'—in hopes of moving on and forgetting as we enter into adulthood. I hope every mom will choose to go with their daughters on these *Adventures with Purity*, receive the life-changing messages, and start a new legacy in the generation coming behind us!"
—*Jenni Oates, mother of Micaiah Joy & Eden Grace*

"*Adventures with Purity* is a beautiful, honest way to open the door to healthy conversation about the challenges faced by young women in our culture today. If we as parents aren't talking to our girls about these issues, someone else will. Bold, yet tasteful, these conversations go beyond the issues, to the heart of how to handle these situations in a godly way. This series is foundational to every young woman today."
—*Krissy Nordhoff, mother of Anthem*

"I have been touched and overwhelmed by the message of *Adventures with Purity*. How I wish I would have had it when I was younger, but I am thrilled it is available for my daughters! *Adventures with Purity* is current, fun, and comforting. The way in which Rebekah Joy depicts various types of girls accurately portrays the reality of what is going on in our culture. So many women of all ages feel condemned, and because they have not yet received grace, they fall into deeper despair that nobody knows about. The message of *Adventures with Purity* is going to help young girls avoid the path that leads to destruction, and save so many others that have continued down that path because they feel condemned already."

—*Brooke Thomas, mother of Reagan & Riley*

"Rebekah Joy has creatively opened the door to many crucial conversations that every mother MUST have with her daughter. *Adventures with Purity* reveals God's unconditional love for us, while also exposing Satan's deceptive, yet subtle, lies in our society. Each adventure addresses real issues that girls in our culture struggle with on a regular basis. With discussion guides and a plan of action at the end of every adventure, talking about difficult topics with our generation of young girls has never been easier!"

—*Rachell Comley, mother of Kaitlyn & Ashlyn*

"*Adventures with Purity* is brilliant for young girls in this age who are faced with extreme challenges to remain pure. Rebekah makes these characters come to life so that readers can easily relate and be educated. I'm looking forward to sharing this with my daughter!"

—*Arlyne VanHook, mother of Madison*

"If ever a book was needed for young women, *Adventures with Purity* is it. Today's culture is saturated with sex and lies, leaving girls young and old with a skewed understanding of healthy and pure living. *Adventures with Purity* is filled with biblical truth and practical examples sure to identify with ALL ages. I cannot think of a better message needed today. Rebekah shares her real life through Purity in a way that leaves you captivated, encouraged, and hopeful. Whether you read it alone or with your youth, just be sure you read it."

—*Makaela Suitt, mother of Lillie*

"Rebekah Joy has taken difficult, real-life issues and opened the door for honest, godly communication between parents and their late tween/early teenage girls. I am grateful for the clarity of the issues and how Rebekah Joy applies God's Word to each one. Let's use these God-inspired adventures to help our girls live the life He intended for them."

—*Michelle Majors, mother of Tiffany & Ambrianna*

"*Adventures with Purity* is a must-read for young girls, moms, and mentors. The journey filled with obstacles, temptations, and desires can be quite inviting. But with Wisdom and Truth by her side, Purity is victorious!"

—*Alyssa Damron, mother of Madison & Emily*

"Rebekah has found a beautiful way to open a conversation that might be uncomfortable to have with the 'daughters' in your life. Purity is a regular girl living an everyday life. The difference for her is that she has a woman who is willing to invest in her life by sharing the truth with her. I would love to see this story impact teenage girls everywhere, and I pray it will open a dialogue that so many need to hear. The gift of your purity is unmatched. Thank you, Rebekah, for sharing your wisdom through this character!"

—*Dina Dell, "bonus" mom of Bree, Madison, Hope, & Noa*

"As a mom of two little girls and one teenage daughter, I have witnessed first-hand how the *great deceiver* (Satan) is on a mission to secretly attack every aspect of young girls' lives, regardless of age. Living in a fallen world where self-indulgence, peer pressure, and false body image is prevalent, girls are being driven away from God's true desire for their lives: *Do not conform to the pattern of this world, but be transformed by the renewing of your mind. Then you will be able to test and approve what is God's will—his good, pleasing and perfect will* (Romans 12:2). *Adventures with Purity* is a book that every mother and daughter should read together!"

—*Michelle Apps, mother of Hailey, Henley, & Hannah*

"*Adventures with Purity* is such a powerful new tool for encouraging our daughters to remain pure in a culture that over-sexualizes females more than ever. As a mother of two girls, I am so excited to have a way to approach this topic with my daughters without it seeming awkward or preachy! Purity shows girls that they can impact their friends, be leaders in their schools, and that it's actually cool to be pure! Rebekah Joy has such a gift for getting on their level and speaking their language. I truly believe the Lord has called her to this field and that she will impact thousands of girls to stand up for their purity in the face of a world that tells them to do the exact opposite."

—*Carrie Layson, mother of Greta & Frances*

Foreword

To be asked to write the forward for this timely and much-needed book is an unexpected honor. I had the privilege of being called alongside Rebekah in a mentoring relationship eight years ago. At that point, she was a wounded, fearful, and hurting young woman. Through what proved to be an uphill climb in more ways than I can count, with God's strong persistence we have held on for dear life and together witnessed the unfolding of a beautiful miracle that God has so graciously fashioned in our lives. I have always known that God had a lofty calling on Rebekah's life, as evidenced by the intense nature of the pathway to her complete wholeness and freedom in Christ—a path that was worn on our knees and through many deep and difficult discussions over God's Word and His heart towards us. And now, eight years later, I get to behold the beauty of God's amazing grace poured sweetly over her life on a continual basis ... past, present, and future.

Thank You God for parting the deep and turbulent waters we have treaded, keeping our heads and our hearts above that water line, and for now opening up the wellspring of life-producing treasures you have forged deep within Rebekah's heart just for us. As with many spiritual mentoring relationships, I have been the most challenged and transformed through these years. I am humbled and honored beyond words to present to you the results and the overflow of what I have personally witnessed God building in Rebekah for the world to receive. You are blessed to hold in your hands what I believe is a complete game-changer for us as parents, mentors, and leaders of the young women we have been called to disciple.

When I read the very first draft of *Adventures with Purity*, I found myself thinking: *If only ... If only something like this had been available when I was a young woman, my life choices and the consequences I experienced could have been so very different.* I regularly hear the fear and concern of Christian parents as it pertains to raising their daughters to be wise, strong, and spiritually healthy in a society that has swung so far away from biblical morality and truth.

Through this timely tool, Rebekah has struck a vital but missing cord in the delicate balance of communication between young women and their parents and mentors. Because of the growing number of difficult life issues our daughters are facing in this post-modern culture, so often we parents, mentors, and youth leaders wrestle with fear and frustration—unsure as to how to effectively and appropriately address the hot topics swirling around our girls today. As a result of this struggle, difficult conversations are all-too-often neglected; therefore, our girls are left to try to figure out life on their own—which can be detrimental.

Adventures with Purity lays the solid groundwork for us and the young women we love. It allows us to unveil the hard issues, confront them with relevant accuracy, and provide a natural and necessary means of dialogue between girls and their parents or leaders that will assist in navigating the cultural minefields we tiptoe through daily.

Through descriptive and allegorical characters, Rebekah captures the authentic reality our girls are exposed to every day. She wraps the sensitive heart and wisdom of God around that reality, giving us all a powerful tool by which to guide our girls specifically and successfully. These short stories will draw you in with accurate familiarity, offering informative truth and wisdom to know how to apply that truth when facing difficult circumstances. As I've read these stories with my own daughter, I have been both grateful and relieved to have a means by which to talk with, guide, and better equip her to avoid the potential pitfalls she may encounter.

Because of Rebekah Joy's offering through *Adventures with Purity*, years from now our daughters are less likely to look back with regret and say, *if only* ...

— *Laura Atkins, May 2013*

Introduction

I am so glad you have chosen to join Purity on what will no doubt prove to be an exciting, challenging, and eye-opening journey! Before you get started, please be aware that every adventure is a stand-alone story. At the end of each one you will find *Thoughts for Reflection & Discussion* as well as *Purity's Plan of Action*. These can be completed individually, with your mom or mentor, or discussed in a small group setting. If you have friends who would like to join Purity on her adventures, read the stories together and then share your thoughts with each other. This is a great way to gain further wisdom, understanding, and encouragement.

Know that you are extremely special and God has incredible plans for your life! He loves you unconditionally, He created you with a unique purpose, and He will fully equip you to live out your destiny.

It is my hope and prayer that through *Adventures with Purity* you encounter grace and freedom, and are further equipped to apply wisdom and truth every day of your life. Remember … apart from Jesus you and I can do nothing. But with Him, nothing is impossible for us!

—*Rebekah Joy*

♥♥♥
A Letter from Purity

Hey there!

My name is Purity and I am so pumped you are along for these adventures. I sure love making new friends!

As you get to know me better, you may discover that we have some things in common. I'm in my last year of middle school, and I love to shop and have sleepovers with my friends. But don't let my painted nails, cool accessories, and super cute outfits fool you. I can also hang with the best of them on the basketball court or soccer field! I guess you could say I'm an all-around girl—a diva by day, and a 'baller' by night ... or at least during practice and games!

Like you, I have lots of dreams for my future. I've thought about being a hair stylist—that seems like a pretty fun career! I'd also like to start my own business. One thing I know for sure is that I totally want to get married someday. How amazing would it be to live life with the man who is my best bud!

My parents told me that I have a God-given treasure called my sexual purity that I get to give my husband on our wedding night. They say my treasure is the absolute best gift I can give him! Actually, my parents named me Purity because they believe purity is a lifestyle that involves my heart and mind, not just my body ... so they wanted my name to reflect that. For now, I am living an awesome, real-life adventure while closely guarding my treasure until it's the right time to give it away.

God has also given you the treasure of your sexual purity! Remember, a treasure is worth much more when it's kept safe. So let's help each other make good choices that protect our bodies, minds, and hearts. I'm up for the challenge if you are!

Throughout these adventures you'll get to meet my best friends, along with other influences like Emotion, Body Image, and Peer Pressure. We're going to have many opportunities to make wise decisions and learn from the experiences of others.

At the end of each adventure there will be a super important letter from my amazing mom, Wisdom. Please be sure to read that because she has some incredible advice for you! I'm pumped that we are on these adventures together. Here we go!

 Purity
XOXO

Purity Discovers Peer Pressure

♥♥♥

"Walk with the wise and become wise;
associate with fools and get in trouble."

~ King Solomon ~

"What's up, girls?" Purity eagerly greeted her friends as she hurried over to the table where they were sitting in the cafeteria.

Summer vacation had just come to an end, which meant Purity and her friends were about to begin their last year of middle school. Students from both the middle and high school were gathered in the cafeteria, preparing to leave on a two-day retreat.

"What are you so excited about?" asked Loyal, Purity's best friend since Kindergarten.

"My mom and I had a really cool talk last night, and I can't wait to hear what you all think about it! Gather 'round, girls!"

Purity, Loyal, and their other friends—Compassion and Patience—huddled together at the end of the table. These girls seemed to always be together.

"Well hurry up and tell us, Purity," urged Compassion. "What did you and your mom talk about that has you so giddy?"

"I have to admit," began Purity, "that at first I was a little nervous when I realized my mom was going to bring up the ... you know ... the sex issue with me again. But she is so cool about everything. It wasn't nearly as awkward as the first time we had 'the talk!'"

"Oh my goodness! I remember when my mom had 'the talk' with me!" exclaimed Patience. "I was totally embarrassed."

"Well, believe it or not, this is nothing to be embarrassed about," Purity stated. "My mom talked with me about the importance of having friends who will encourage me to do what is right—especially in the area of staying pure sexually. She called it *Peer Pressure* ... and said that means my friends will either impact me for good or for bad."

"I've heard of that before," said Loyal. "One of our teachers talked about Peer Pressure. She said the friends we choose will totally influence the choices we make every day."

"Purity, did your mom give you any examples from her own life?" asked Patience. "Did she tell you what kinds of friends she had when she was our age?"

"Yes—she told me lots of stories," responded Purity. "I love hearing about her younger days. But the best part was that she gave me an idea I think we should go ahead and try out now!"

"What's that?" asked Compassion. "And do we have time?"

"Sure we do," said Patience. "They're still waiting on the rest of the students to arrive; then they have to finish getting the luggage packed in the vans."

"Awesome!" Purity exclaimed. "My mom said it might help us learn a lot if we could find some older girls to talk to about Peer Pressure. Maybe we could ask them what they think about friends being able to influence each other." Purity glanced across the room and continued talking. "Do you all see those girls sitting in the far corner?"

"Yes," the other three responded in unison.

"I think they are in eleventh grade," continued Purity. "I bet they'd be great to hang out with for a few minutes. If nothing else, maybe they have experienced some of the things we've been talking about."

"I don't know," said Patience. "Those girls look a little intimidating to me. Do you think they'd even want to be seen with us? After all, we are several years younger than them."

"Don't be scared," Purity encouraged. "We need to hear what they have to say about all this. Come on—let's go!"

Purity, ever the fearless leader, marched over to the table where four older girls sat. Loyal, Patience, and Compassion followed close behind—still a bit unsure, but gaining courage because of Purity's boldness.

Upon arriving, Purity introduced herself and her friends. "We'd like to ask you all some questions if you don't mind," said Purity. "But first, could you tell us your names?"

One of the older girls spoke up: "Okay—we don't mind answering your questions. My name is Wounded." She proceeded to go around the table and introduce the other girls. "This is Regret. That's Ashamed. And beside me is Used. We've hung out for the past year or so now. So what do you want to know?"

"Thanks so much for taking time for us," said Purity. "We've been talking about Peer Pressure, especially when it comes to staying pure sexually. My mom said the friends we choose to hang out with will influence us either positively or negatively. We'd really like to know what you all think."

Compassion couldn't help but notice the sadness that came over Wounded's face as she started to answer Purity's question. "Well, I can't speak for the others," began Wounded, "but I would have to say a huge *yes*—your friends certainly do influence you, whether you realize it or not."

"I learned that lesson the hard way," continued Wounded. "I used to hang out with an older girl named Rebellion. She convinced me that my parents did not know what they were talking about, and that the rules they set for me were far too strict. I felt bad disobeying my parents, but one night Rebellion talked me into sneaking out of my house. It was the only time I ever snuck out, but that was all it took for my life to be changed forever."

Purity, Loyal, Patience, and Compassion sat wide-eyed as they listened to Wounded share her story.

"Rebellion drove me to a party where there were lots of good-looking older guys. One of them named Lust started paying a lot of attention to me. His interest made me feel special at first, but after a while, the way he looked at me caused me to be uncomfortable. He asked me to go hang out in a room upstairs. I went with him, not realizing we were going to be the only ones in the room. Before I could really think about what was happening, Lust had taken my purity—one of my most precious and valuable treasures, and there was nothing

I could do to get it back. I knew right away that I had lost something very special."

Wounded wiped away a tear, then continued: "Rebellion drove me back home that night—I cried the whole way. She never spoke to me again. I'm not sure why Rebellion was so angry with me. About two weeks after the night of the party, I saw Lust in the hallway at school. He just glared at me like I was the one who had done something horribly wrong. I never told my parents about what happened because they didn't even know I was at the party."

"Wow," said Compassion, shocked and saddened by what she was hearing.

"I agree with Wounded," Ashamed said softly. Purity and the others had to scoot closer to hear Ashamed, because she spoke quietly and never looked up at them. "I got involved with the wrong group of girls. They go to a different school now, so I don't feel bad for telling you their names. My closest friend at that time was Immodest. We also hung out with Revealing and Seductive. My mother tried to tell me that the way those girls dressed was attracting the wrong kind of attention from boys. She didn't know that I also dressed like them. I would wear outfits my mom approved of until I got to school, but then I would go to the bathroom and change into the skimpier clothes I had in my backpack. At the time, I thought I was so smart. But I see now that I would have kept my heart from a lot of pain if I had only followed my mom's advice."

Ashamed's shoulders seemed to droop lower and lower as she spoke. "I should have chosen friends who would have influenced me to dress stylishly, yet modestly," she continued.

"Unfortunately, my choice of clothing was what attracted Player, the guy who smooth-talked me into giving him the treasure of my purity. I don't think that ever would've happened had Player not already thought I wanted to give my treasure away ... based on the revealing clothes I wore."

"I am so sorry," said Compassion. "You girls don't have to tell us anymore if you don't want to. We don't want you to feel bad by talking about the past."

"It's alright," chimed in Regret. "I just wish I could be you all's age again and have another shot at this. I promise you I'd choose differently. You girls would be wise to listen to your mothers, aunts, older sisters, or others who want to be positive influences in your life. My mom talked to me several times about Peer Pressure. She warned me that I needed to choose friends who were making wise decisions, but I thought I knew better than her. It turned out that my mom was right. I sure wish I had done what she encouraged me to do."

"Yeah, I agree with Regret," said Used. "Unfortunately all of us so wanted to be accepted by the friends we used to hang out with, that we did things we now wish we wouldn't have. We ended up losing those friends anyway."

"Sometimes my heart hurts so bad I don't know if the pain will ever go away," said Wounded, as she wiped away more tears.

"Yours too?" asked Used. "I thought I was the only one who felt that way. I also feel dirty—like I'm second-hand now. I messed up with an older guy named Flattery. He followed me around for several weeks at school, telling me how pretty

I was, and how he would love to spend forever with me. Well, after Flattery convinced me to give him my treasure, he disappeared. I've not seen or talked to him since then. Now I feel like a dirty rag ... used, tossed to the side, and completely forgotten."

"I'm not sure what to say," said Purity. "I don't think any of us were expecting to hear all this when we came over to talk with you girls."

"You don't have to say anything," said Regret. "We just hope you will learn from our mistakes and choose differently so you don't have to experience the pain each of us have lived with. It sounds like you girls are a great support for each other. It's so important to have friends who will encourage you to make wise choices."

"Thank you all so much for your honesty, and for talking with us," said Patience. "We hope you have a great time on the retreat!"

Purity, Loyal, Patience, and Compassion smiled and headed back to their table.

"Wow! What did you all think about that?" Purity asked.

Patience spoke up first. "Well I don't know about the rest of you, but I thought all those girls looked so sad."

"I agree," said Loyal. "Did you notice that one girl, Used? Her eyes seemed really empty. And Ashamed wouldn't even look at us when she talked."

"I noticed something else too," said Compassion. "Did you all hear what Wounded and Ashamed told us? It's just like your mom said, Purity. Those girls became exactly like the friends they chose to hang out with! Wounded turned out to be like Rebellion, and Ashamed became like Immodest, Revealing, and Seductive."

"Well, I guess we've seen how friends can influence us in the wrong way," said Purity. "Are you all up for talking to another group of older girls, to see if we get a different response?"

"Sure!" chimed in the other three. "It can't get any sadder than what we've already heard," added Loyal.

"Here we go then," said Purity, as she led the group to yet another table of older girls. "I think we still have a few minutes before we are supposed to leave."

Once again Purity introduced herself and her friends, and asked these girls the same questions she'd asked the previous group.

"We are glad you came to talk to us," said one of the girls. "I'll start." She introduced herself as "Committed," then went on to introduce the other girls at the table: "Selfless, Forgiven, and Second Chance."

"I noticed you all were talking with Wounded and her group of friends," said Selfless. "How did that conversation go?"

"Well, honestly, it was kind of discouraging," Loyal responded. "They were nice to answer our questions and tell us the painful truth, but they all seemed so sad and hopeless."

"You are right," Forgiven said. "They have chosen to live in the disappointment and shame of their decisions. I am sad for them, but it is their choice. Regret used to be my best friend. I too made a costly decision when I gave my treasure to the boyfriend I was dating at the time. But then I realized that Jesus still loves me, in spite of my poor choices. When I chose to accept His forgiveness and grace, Regret no longer wanted to hang out with me. It is still a bit awkward at events like this retreat because she completely avoids me."

"I used to be really close with Ashamed," said Second Chance. "When we both made the mistake of messing around with our boyfriends, she got caught in a downward spiral of shame and guilt. I was not proud of the choices I'd made, but I knew that God offered me the hope of another opportunity to do it right the next time. And so far, as I have relied on Him to help me, I have listened to wisdom and made better decisions! Ashamed can't even bring herself to talk to me. I hope that one day she will realize God has given her another chance, just as He did for me. God doesn't condemn her, but unfortunately she still condemns herself."

"That's interesting," said Compassion, "because you both made similar choices as Wounded, Regret, Ashamed, and Used—yet you sure seem a lot happier than they do."

"God's perfect plan is that we save the treasure of our purity for our husband, within the boundary of marriage," explained Second Chance. "If we stray from that plan, there are certainly going to be heartaches and consequences. Yet, as I have experienced, when we come to God receiving His forgiveness, His love and grace give us the opportunity to start over. We do not deserve this, but that's what makes His grace so amazing."

"Forgiven and Second Chance, you are both certainly more encouraging to talk to than Wounded and her friends," said Purity. "I wish that they could experience what you have. What about the two of you, Committed and Selfless—do you have anything to add?"

Committed responded first: "I would say the best decision I ever made in regards to this area was when I was the same age as you girls. It was then that I came up with a plan of how, with God's help, I wanted to protect and save my treasure until it was time to give it to my husband on our wedding night. My plan started with writing a letter that told him of the commitment I had made to save all of myself for him and him alone. That includes letting my future husband be the only guy to ever kiss me. So … my first kiss will be on my wedding day! No matter how many years it is before I get married, I intend to give this letter to my husband on our wedding night."

"That is awesome!" exclaimed Patience. "What a great idea!"

"Committed's advice is pretty amazing," said Selfless. "When Committed told me about her letter, it inspired me to write a letter to my future husband as well. I cannot wait to give it to him one day! Sometimes when the pressure to give away the treasure of my purity gets too strong, I think about my letter. Then I am quickly reminded that I'd much rather wait for God's best, than give in to a few moments of pleasure."

Selfless paused, allowing her words to sink in with the younger girls. "That is the biggest encouragement I could pass on to you. Offering the treasure of your purity before marriage has become normal in our culture, but that has never been God's plan ... even if you don't *go all the way,* as some people like to say. When you make the choice to save it all, giving your treasure to your husband will be far more satisfying."

"Daily living out that decision is not easy," added Committed. "But you girls have taken a big step in the right direction by surrounding yourselves with friends who offer you positive Peer Pressure. That means they encourage and influence you to make decisions you will not regret later. Even though your friends won't always be with you, Jesus will be. He is the One Who gives you strength to resist in a moment of temptation. If you ask Him for it, God promises to give you wisdom so that you will know how to avoid risky situations."

"That is very helpful to know. Thank you all so much!" said Loyal. "We're glad you were willing to talk with and encourage us."

"And one more thing," said Committed as Purity and her friends stood up. "I want to make sure you girls know that there are many amazing guys out there who also believe in the importance of saving their treasure. Every guy is not like Lust, Player, or Flattery. We hang out with a group of guys whose names are Integrity, Courage, and Respect. They are like brothers to us. We have tons of fun with them, and they always honor and protect us."

"Now that's some good news," said Patience. "We'll be on the lookout for guy friends like you described. Thanks again!"

Purity and her friends walked back to their table more lighthearted than before. When they arrived, Purity spoke up: "I don't know about you girls, but when we get on the van, I'm going to start writing my letter!"

"Me too!" the other girls said at once, not yet realizing the powerful impact those conversations would have on their actions for years to come.

A Tish of Truth

King Solomon, one of the wisest men to ever live, once said: *Walk with the wise and become wise; associate with fools and get in trouble.* Solomon understood the importance of choosing friends who were committed to doing what was right. This same principle still applies to you today. Choose friends who will encourage you to make wise decisions, because you tend to become like the people you hang around.

Hey again—it's Purity! Thanks for joining me on this exciting adventure. I want to introduce you to Wisdom, my amazing mom. She has some important thoughts to share with you, so be sure and pay attention to her advice. Trust me … she knows what she is talking about. When I follow what she says, my life seems to go a lot better than when I do what I think is best. Listen closely … you'll be glad you did!

♥ *Purity*
XOXO

♥♥♥
Words of Wisdom

Hi Friend!

Purity and I are so excited you chose to be a part this adventure. We hope Purity's discovery of Peer Pressure helped you see the importance of choosing friends who will influence you in positive ways.

It seems to be human nature to want a step-by-step plan for success. When we follow the steps, we tend to feel good about ourselves. But when we get off track, our minds may experience attacks of guilt and shame, which is exactly what happened to Wounded, Ashamed, Regret, and Used.

For that reason, I want to be sure you understand where to find power to live victoriously. Purity and her friends have given you some awesome advice. Yet if you simply attempt to follow their advice in your own willpower and determination, you may become frustrated and tempted to quit.

So I'd like to introduce you to Grace and Condemnation. You might already be familiar with Condemnation. That's a big word to describe the negative, critical voice you may sometimes hear in your mind. Wounded, Ashamed, Regret, and Used unfortunately chose to listen to the voice of Condemnation, which says things like: *You messed up again. You won't ever get it right. You're a loser. You might as well give up now. You'll never be good enough.* Does that voice sound familiar to you?

On the other hand, Grace is a person: God's Son, Jesus Christ. He loves you so much that He gave His life for you by dying on a cross for all the times you would ever sin or make a mistake. Jesus took the punishment that you deserved. While on the cross, Jesus was condemned in your place so that you would no longer have to listen to the voice of Condemnation. Jesus defeated sin and death by coming back to life three days after He died! You can experience Grace today simply by receiving the gift of salvation through Jesus Christ. Because Forgiven and Second Chance chose Grace, their lives were completely transformed. They didn't stay under the hindering grip of shame and guilt.

How is Grace different from Condemnation? While Condemnation points a finger and accuses you, Grace lovingly puts an arm around you and says: *You made a mistake? That's okay. If you have received the salvation Jesus offers, you are under the continual waterfall of Grace washing over you. Grace cleanses you from any and every sin, so don't dwell on the mistake. The more you think about a mistake, the more likely you are to continue struggling in that area. But when you focus on Grace and what Jesus has done for you, you will have more than enough power to live victoriously.* Grace brings life to your heart; Condemnation brings death. Wouldn't you rather listen to the kind voice of Grace instead of the harsh voice of Condemnation?

Our culture loves the idea of superheroes—those larger-than-life beings that have extraordinary abilities. Well ... Jesus is not that kind of superhero, but He is certainly supernatural! That means He has divine power to do incredible works that neither you nor I can possibly do in our own strength. The good news is that when you receive Jesus as your Savior, His power then equips you to do mighty works too! I Corinthians

10:13 tells you that *God is faithful. He will not allow the temptation to be more than you can stand. When you are tempted, he will show you a way out.* This is how Committed and Selfless have been able to resist temptation and guard the treasure of their purity. Their confidence is in God, not themselves.

Jesus now lives in heaven with His Father, so God sent His Spirit to be with us here on earth. When you receive the free gift of Grace, the Spirit of God comes to live within you, and is available to be your Source of wisdom and power so you can live victoriously!

So Friend, whatever issue you are struggling with, I encourage you to stop trying to overcome it in your own limited abilities. That will only lead to further frustration and defeat. As you rely on Grace and strength through the power of the Spirit, you can be triumphant over all of life's challenges.

If you have never before received the gift of Jesus as your Savior, you can do so today. There is no need to be nervous. Talking to God is no different than talking to a friend. God loves you unconditionally and desires a relationship with you. That is the greatest gift ever offered. When you receive it, you will then have supernatural power to apply the advice Purity and her friends have shared with you!

Purity and I are so proud of you!

Wisdom

A Prayer to Receive Grace

Dear Jesus, I have been listening to the voice of Condemnation for too long. I know that I cannot be victorious in this life by relying on my own abilities. Today I receive the free gift of Grace that comes through You alone. I acknowledge that I am a sinner and I receive You, Jesus, as my Savior—the payment for my sins. Thank You that Grace cleanses me once and for all. Though I may still make mistakes, I do not have to live under Condemnation any longer because You have already forgiven me. Today I receive Grace and Your Spirit's wisdom and power that equip me to live victoriously. Thank You for these amazing gifts!

Thoughts for Reflection & Discussion

1) What qualities do you look for when choosing your friends?

2) What kind of influence are your friends on you? How do they dress? What do they talk about? Does the music they listen to communicate positive or negative messages?

3) When has a friend persuaded you to do something you knew was wrong? What were the consequences?

4) How have *you* influenced your friends to make good decisions?

5) Of the first group of older girls Purity and her friends talked to, which one impacted you the most and why?

6) Do any of your friends encourage you to protect and save the treasure of your purity? Which one(s)?

7) Have you ever met Rebellion? Was she able to convince you that her way was better than the guidelines your parents/authority figures had put in place for your protection? What happened as a result of your following Rebellion?

8) If you have encountered Lust, Player, or Flattery, how did you feel around them?

9) Have you ever met Immodest, Revealing, or Seductive? Were you tempted to dress and act the way they do?

10) How were Forgiven and Second Chance (from the second group of older girls) different than Wounded, Regret, Ashamed, and Used?

11) What stood out to you about Committed and Selfless? Do you agree or disagree with their advice? Why?

12) Why is it unwise to offer parts of your treasure to random guys along the way (Example: kissing every guy you date)?

13) Do you have any guy friends who treat you with honor and protect you the way Integrity, Courage, and Respect did for the second group of older girls? Do your guy friends value the treasure of their purity and yours?

Purity's Plan of Action

♥ Take some time to carefully consider Committed's advice: *I came up with a plan of how, with God's help, I wanted to protect and save my treasure until it was time to give it to my husband on our wedding night. My plan started with writing a letter that told him of the commitment I had made to save all of myself for him and him alone.* Now it's your turn to establish a very clear plan for how you intend to guard and protect the treasure of your purity. Ask your parents or a trusted older friend or sibling to help you; they may have some valuable insights and advice to offer. Remember, a plan is much more than signing a pledge or wearing a "purity ring". Those symbols of your heart-felt commitment will do little to help you in a moment of temptation. You need to decide in advance specific guidelines for keeping your treasure safe. Here are some sample questions to answer:

o Will I be alone with a guy for any reason? Group dates and double-dating are fun and wise alternatives!

o Does my choice of clothing show that I respect myself and the guys around me?

o Who in my life will I ask to keep me accountable and help me guard my treasure?

o Understanding that purity is a lifestyle that stems from what goes into my heart and mind, what will I watch, read, look at, and listen to?

♥ If you have already given away parts of your treasure, today is a perfect day to start over. Remember the words of Second Chance: *I was not proud of the choices I'd made, but I knew that God offered me the hope of another opportunity to do it right the next time. And so far, as I have relied on Him to help me, I have made better decisions!* How are you going to guard your purity from this moment forward?

♥ When you are ready, go ahead and write a letter to your future husband. Be sure to put the date—and you might even want to include a picture of yourself! When you are done, stick it in an envelope, write *Husband* on the outside, and put it in a very safe place. This letter, and all the years of saving your treasure, will be an amazing gift for your future husband on your wedding day!

Purity's Spa Night with Wisdom

♥♥♥

"For wisdom is far more valuable than rubies.
Nothing you desire can compare with it."

~ King Solomon ~

"I'm finished with my homework, Mom!" called out Purity. "Is it time to give each other manicures and pedicures?"

"It sure is," Wisdom enthusiastically responded. "I've been looking forward to our date all day! Come join me on the back porch; we'll sit out here a while."

Purity headed to the screened-in back porch where her mother had everything ready for their spa night. "I'm so excited for you to do my nails! I'd like a French manicure please," said Purity.

"I've never seen you so eager to get your nails done! What's up with that?"

"I'm just happy about getting to hang out with you and have you all to myself," Purity confessed. "I love it when we chat because you like to hear my stories about school and friends, and you always tell me important things I need to know."

"I'm so grateful to have a daughter who listens and applies what she hears!" answered Wisdom. "Not every young woman your age cares to spend time with her mom—or pay attention to what she says."

Wisdom motioned for Purity to sit down, so she could start on her manicure.

"So ... what do you want to talk about?" asked Purity.

"I'd like to share some things with you that you will likely encounter sooner or later. Honestly Purity, I wish I'd had a head's up about these issues—it certainly would have equipped me to handle many situations differently."

"Am I in trouble?" Purity nervously asked.

"Of course not!" Wisdom responded. "I just love you and know that our talk tonight is going to help prepare you for your future."

"Wow, Mom. Thanks for caring enough to talk with me. It really does show how much you love me."

"Remember how I've always told you that *what goes in will eventually come out?*" asked Wisdom.

"Of course I do. It seems like you say that to me nearly every day!"

"Well there is a reason for that, Purity. You are constantly being bombarded by Media and Entertainment ..."

"Excuse me, Mom. I'm sorry to interrupt you, but who or what exactly are Media and Entertainment?"

"I'm glad you asked because it's very important that you understand this. Media and Entertainment are basically any communication tool that is capable of spreading a message— you know, like television, radio, the Internet, movies, magazines, and newspapers."

"Okay—that makes sense."

"Every day Media and Entertainment offer you cleverly designed advertisements and messages in an effort to sell you on a certain way to dress, carry yourself, act around the opposite sex, and so much more. They use the avenue of mass communication—including social media—to reach large numbers of people."

"Seriously, Mom—I totally get what you're saying. There are lots of girls at school who talk way too much about the clothes and jewelry Celebrity wears, what kind of purse Celebrity carries, and who Celebrity is dating. Then they try to copy what they see Celebrity doing in the movies and magazines."

"Why do you think they copy Celebrity?" asked Wisdom.

"I guess just because they want to fit in. I don't know any other reason they would go to all that trouble. But it's impossible to keep up because Celebrity always has a new purse, the latest phone, and perfect fashion for every season. It seems like that way of living would get really tiring—not to mention expensive!"

"You're absolutely right, Purity. No matter how young or old they are, most women want to fit in and be accepted. But unfortunately, far too many are wearing themselves out as they try to keep up with Celebrity. There are other reasons as well."

"Like what?" asked Purity.

"Well … many of the messages communicated by Media and Entertainment are designed to program our minds for a certain response to what we are seeing and hearing. I want to tell you about two of those responses."

"I'm all ears, Mom!"

"The first is Greed, which causes us to feel an urgency that we just 'have to have' what all the 'cool' people have. Greed often teams up with Self-Centered to keep our minds focused on what we think will make *us* the happiest. You've heard the phrase *looking out for number one* ... that comes from Greed and Self-Centered. Many poor and costly decisions have been made because a person allowed Greed and Self-Centered to influence their actions—even if just for a moment."

"I can think of plenty examples in my own life. So what's the second response that Media and Entertainment program us for?" asked Purity.

"Desensitization."

"Now that's a monster of a word. What does it mean?"

"You've heard the story about how to cook a frog," began Wisdom. "You put a frog in water and then gradually increase the heat until it's boiling. Even though the water has been getting hotter and hotter, the frog won't jump out—even after the water starts to boil!"

"But if you put a frog in water that's already boiling," interrupted Purity, "it will jump right out!"

"So what's the point of that story?" asked Wisdom.

"It's an example of something very dangerous slowly happening—and the frog didn't notice until it was too late."

"Exactly! And that's a great way to describe desensitization … when we gradually come to accept actions, words, and ideas that we know are wrong, but we've been steadily conditioned to believe they are okay."

"I get that," said Purity.

"An example that deals specifically with Media and Entertainment is that not too many years ago, it would have caused an uproar for same-sex couples to appear on a television show." Wisdom paused before continuing. "But Media and Entertainment began by introducing a scene or two, then a character, and now, entire television series are built around same-sex couples … and we think that's normal! Even if we say we're opposed to the messages Media and Entertainment are promoting, our actions prove otherwise."

"How so?" asked Purity.

"Because we still watch the television shows, pay to see the movies, and purchase and listen to the music. That's Desensitization."

"Oh wow—I get your point. So if we're not careful about what we watch, listen to, and look at, then we might have that happen to us, almost without even realizing it. That's actually kind of scary."

"Yes it is," responded Wisdom. "Another way to think of Desensitization is that it's a slow numbing process in which we no longer feel a reaction to things that we should be very concerned about. Some other examples include overly violent movies and video games; the devaluing of human life through mistreating the elderly and unborn; common use of inappropriate language; and high sexual content—things that used to be treasured and kept private are now done in front of huge audiences. And as I said before, we have come to accept this as normal. From same-sex couples to teenagers having sex to couples living together before marriage … these actions no longer bother us. And yes, Purity, that is scary. Our culture is rapidly declining by way of our morals and values. Most people don't realize we are paying a high price for our *new normals*."

Purity listened closely as Wisdom continued: "No matter which direction you look—whether to television, movies, magazines, music, billboards, or the Internet, more than likely you are going to see an advertisement that in some way contains pictures of outwardly beautiful people who appear to be having the time of their life by using a certain product or believing a new idea. The message being communicated is that you can be happy too, if you'll just buy the product or accept the idea they are promoting. Have you ever noticed how the catchy words and tunes you hear on these ads replay in your mind over and over—even when you're *not* trying to remember them?"

"Oh yeah … that happens to me a lot," responded Purity. "I hear a song once or twice, and then it seems like I can't stop singing it."

"But it's a big reason why I tell you that *what goes in will eventually come out*! If you allow certain images, lyrics, and songs to enter your mind and heart, sooner or later they will resurface in some way—perhaps even through your actions. That's why King Solomon said to *guard your heart.*"

"I know what you mean, Mom ... and by the way, my nails are looking great!"

"I'm glad you like them!" said Wisdom.

"There is no doubt that Celebrity and others similar to her are extremely talented. But all-too-often the messages they speak, sing, or promote in other ways—like how they dress—are not beneficial. The sad part is that some of them have millions of fans and followers, yet they are not using their influence wisely."

"That is so true. At school a couple days ago some girls were talking about how Celebrity has over 50 million *likes* on Facebook and more than 30 million *followers* on Twitter! That's a lot of people!"

"It sure is. All the more reason for Celebrity to be wise with words and pictures she posts or tweets—but unfortunately that's not always the case. Purity, even at your age you have already been gifted with influence. You have friends that look up to you, and whether you realize it or not, people are always watching you. Every word you speak and every action you take is noticed by someone. That's not meant to put pressure on you, but it is a necessary reminder."

"I understand. You and Dad have always told me not to try by my own efforts ..."

"… because that only leads to frustration," added Wisdom. "But when we rely on God's grace, He gives wisdom and His Spirit empowers us to make good decisions that will be a positive influence for others."

"I've experienced that a lot at school actually. It's pretty cool when I ask God what to do and then I hear the solution."

"That's awesome! I am so proud of you!" Wisdom paused from the manicure long enough to take a quick drink.

"Now … this next topic might seem a bit heavy, but it may already be happening with girls in your class so it's important that we talk about it. Pay close attention, okay Purity? And be sure to stop me if you have questions."

"I will, Mom."

"We've talked before about the warning found in 1 Peter 5:8-9 which says: *Stay alert! Watch out for your great enemy, the devil. He prowls around like a roaring lion, looking for someone to devour. Stand firm against him, and be strong in your faith.* We know that when Jesus died on the cross and rose from the grave, He was victorious over sin and the devil. But even though the devil has been forever defeated, he still fights and attempts to take as many people down with him as possible."

"Which is why Peter told us to *stay alert* and *watch out*," said Purity.

"That's exactly right. Satan—*the one deceiving the whole world*—absolutely hates females for two main reasons: our ability to produce Life, and the beauty we carry that reflects the beauty of God. For now we're going to focus on that first one. God designed us females with the ability to mother and give Life—whether that be through birthing a child of our own, or in numerous other ways we can offer Life to those in need."

"Like how?" asked Purity.

"Through our presence, a hug, a listening ear, or a word of advice," answered Wisdom. "Other ways might be through accepting someone who feels like an outcast ... or through a powerful idea the Holy Spirit births in us and brings to Life through us."

"That makes sense. I guess I never realized a woman can give Life in more ways than just having children!"

"On the other hand, Jesus called Satan *a murderer from the beginning ... a liar and the father of lies*. So notice the drastic difference ... females were created to be mothers and bring Life, while Satan chose to be the father of deception and source of much death. Because he hates women, Life, and ultimately he hates the God Whose image we are made in, this master deceiver has launched an all-out war on women— to trick us into being *life-takers* instead of *life-givers*."

"Yikes! You're talking about Abortion, aren't you?" Purity asked.

"Yes I am," Wisdom answered.

"I've heard some of the older girls at school mention it before. They said Abortion is a convenient way for a woman to end her pregnancy if she isn't ready to be pregnant."

"That's exactly why I knew you and I needed to have this heart-to-heart ... to be sure you understand exactly what Abortion is. At its core, Abortion is both a spirit of death and a spirit of murder."

"Whoa ... that seems pretty intense—a lot different than how the girls at school made is sound."

"It is, Purity. Saying that Abortion is simply a *way to end a pregnancy* is not telling the full truth. I know it sounds harsh, but Abortion is literally killing an unborn child. Since our government legalized Abortion in 1973, 55 million unborn babies have been brutally murdered. That decision has wiped out a generation and caused a depth of pain and regret that most are unwilling to acknowledge."

"55 million? That's awful!" Purity's face showed a mixture of shock and sadness. "It's hard to even imagine a number that big ... or that many people. I remember one day in History class we talked about the Holocaust; that was when six million Jews were killed under Hitler's rule."

"You make a very good point," said Wisdom. "But as horrible as the Holocaust was, through legalized Abortion, Americans have cut short millions more innocent lives than Hitler did."

"I don't understand why Hitler's actions are in my textbook, but Abortion is not."

"Strange isn't it. There were approximately one million Jewish children who were murdered during the Holocaust—that's *54 million less than* the number of children who have died under the so-called *freedom of choice* our leaders have allowed. Those same leaders would likely say Hitler's actions were cruel and barbaric. Yet somehow they justify killing the unborn."

"That just doesn't make any sense. Why do women even choose Abortion?" asked Purity.

"I believe fear is a major reason—especially for teenage girls who are still in school and perhaps not even old enough to drive. The thought of being pregnant and not knowing how their parents, friends, and teachers will respond can be very frightening. And for a girl who's your age, Purity, the thought of being a mother would no doubt be quite scary—especially if she hasn't told anyone and is trying to process through that on her own. Girls who have grown up in a religious home may unfortunately fear being judged or looked down upon if people know they are pregnant; so Abortion can seem like the only way out."

"I cannot imagine a girl my age making that big of a decision because she was afraid. That's so sad." Wisdom noticed tears filling up Purity's big blue eyes.

"Many teenage girls and women have chosen Abortion simply because they were unaware of the truth. They believed the lies that are often spread through Media and Entertainment, telling women that what's growing inside them is not really a person, but rather a blob of tissue. Purity, that is a lie straight from hell—you know that, right?"

"Absolutely. Life begins at conception—God says that He *knit me together in my mother's womb* … that means I was developing and growing while I was inside you—which wouldn't have been possible if I had just been a non-living blob of tissue."

"That's very true," said Wisdom. "For the most part, Media and Entertainment tell women that Abortion is simply an option of convenience ... implying that having a baby is inconvenient, so the solution is to get rid of what is considered to have been a mistake. But the truth is that no pregnancy is ever a *mistake.*

"Purity, I want to make something extremely clear to you. At some point you will no doubt meet women who have experienced Abortion. It's incredibly important that you show compassion and grace to them. Satan—the enemy—doesn't play fair. He loves to tempt unmarried girls and women into having pre-marital sex. Then when they get pregnant, he tricks them into choosing Abortion. After that, he turns and points a finger of condemnation at them. The enemy tries to keep them under intense guilt and shame so that they'll never tell anyone their secret. What they most need is to understand that God offers forgiveness for the choice they made—all they have to do is receive His grace and forgiveness, and allow Him to begin healing their heart."

"Are you telling me all that because some people aren't nice to women who have experienced Abortion?" asked Purity.

"Well, unfortunately there can be a tendency to judge those who we consider to have done something worse than what we've done. We humans often put sins in categories like not-too-bad, kind-of-bad, and really-bad—but God doesn't do that. Sin is sin. Because of sin, each of us is in desperate need of a Savior."

"I know I've done that many times," said Purity. "I guess if I were honest, the main reason I would compare someone else's sins to mine is just to try and make myself feel better if my actions didn't seem as bad as theirs."

"That is a very powerful insight, Purity. Many adults don't even realize they are doing the very thing you just described. Now let's say a 16 year-old girl whom we'll call *Afraid* lied to her teacher about having done her homework. Afraid also had sex with her boyfriend, got pregnant, and chose Abortion. What is your reaction to her choices?"

"Well, it's normal to think that choosing Abortion was worse than telling a lie—but like you said, to God all sin is equal. So really in His eyes, a lie is no different than Abortion—right?"

"That's exactly right. However ... it is extremely important to understand that while sin is sin, some sins or poor choices carry much stronger consequences than others."

"I'm all ears, Mom," encouraged Purity.

"I would imagine that when Afraid's teacher finds out she lied about her homework, more-than-likely Afraid will receive a '0' for that assignment and her mom will get a phone call from the teacher. But a choice like Abortion results in far greater consequences that may torment Afraid and negatively impact all areas of her life unless she receives healing."

"Really?" asked Purity. "I knew Abortion was not a good choice for the baby, but I've never heard anyone talk about women needing healing for it."

"Abortion goes against the very nature of how God designed a woman—which is to *give Life*, as we talked about earlier. So when a woman's body has begun the process of growing Life, but then that natural process is cut short in a very unnatural way, what she experiences is extremely traumatic—for her physical body, her emotions, her mind, her spiritual well-being, and her relationships. Every part of her is negatively affected by Abortion."

"Wow ... I didn't realize that," responded Purity ... clearly shocked by the reality of what she was hearing. "Abortion is definitely *not* just a way to end a pregnancy—like those older girls at school said it was."

"Purity, I know many women who have chosen Abortion. I also know women who got pregnant unexpectedly but chose to give birth to their child. Both of those decisions drastically changed these women's lives. But of those I have personally known, not one single woman says they are glad they chose Abortion. Every one of them has experienced deep pain and regret. On the other hand, I don't know of any women who chose Life that wish they'd chosen Abortion instead."

"So clearly Life is the best choice," said Purity.

"Absolutely," responded Wisdom. "And there is more than one way to choose Life. Some women—especially teenage girls, realize that they are not yet prepared to be a mother, and are unable to provide all that their child needs. So they choose Life by first giving birth, and then by choosing Adoption. This is an incredibly difficult and heart-wrenching decision that likely comes with many tears. But it's made by loving mothers who simply want the best for their child."

"That's a lot to take in," Purity responded. "I am so sad for all the ladies who have chosen Abortion ... and even for the ones who chose Adoption—I cannot imagine how hard it was for them to say good-bye to their babies. But like you said, they did it out of love and believed another family could better care for their child."

"Even though Media and Entertainment say Abortion is a good option, in my eyes, Adoption is the only other *life-giving* option a woman has. Abortion is the counterfeit."

"What do you mean by that, Mom?" asked Purity.

"You tell me," responded Wisdom. "How did God choose to make us His daughters?"

"Through adopting us into His family."

"Exactly! So clearly Adoption is very close to His heart. That's another reason why the enemy tries so hard to make women think Abortion is their only choice. He knows that every time a woman lovingly chooses Adoption, a life is saved and much heartache is avoided. Abortion results in death and pain. Adoption results in Life and joy."

"If I hear those girls at school talking about Abortion again, I'm going to tell them about Adoption," said Purity. "They definitely need to know the difference."

"Yes, they do. Abortion is heartbreaking for the children whose lives were cut short, and also for the teenage girls and women who are left to cope with or cover up a decision that forever changed their lives. God loves these women immensely, and He wants them to be healed."

"I sure hope they know that God isn't mad at them."

"I agree with you, Purity. And we have the opportunity to extend God's love to them."

"Really? How so?"

"It is believed that one out of every three or four women will choose Abortion in their lifetime ... so it's very likely that we are often around these hurting women without even realizing it. God can use us to bring Life to them. Always be sensitive to Him ... He'll tell you who needs a hug, an encouraging word, or a listening ear."

"I will, Mom. I don't like the thought of anyone being sad and hurting—even if they are all smiles on the outside."

Somewhere in the midst of the conversation, Wisdom had finished Purity's manicure. Both were content to simply sit and chat; the pedicures could wait for another day.

"Look me in the eyes, Purity," Wisdom said as she leaned forward in her chair so her face was just inches away from Purity's. "I believe you are a young woman who is going to make wise decisions and save the treasure of your sexual purity until your wedding night. But if something ever happened and you got pregnant, promise me that you would tell your Dad and me so we could work through it together. Abortion is absolutely never to be considered as an option—understood?"

"I promise, Mom—but you don't have to worry about that ever happening."

"I'm not worried; I just know that so many young women who find out they're pregnant choose Abortion in large part because they are afraid of telling their parents. That should never ever be a fear for you.

"Purity, God designed you to be a life-giver, so *always choose Life*. No matter how scary the situation may be, Life is the best choice. No pregnancy is ever a mistake; many are unplanned to the men and women involved, but *none* are a mistake. God has a special plan and purpose for every human life that is conceived. Take Football Player for example … doctors encouraged his mother to choose Abortion because they said the pregnancy could be a risk to her health—but she trusted God and chose Life. Football Player has become an incredible role model in this generation—for young and old alike."

"OMG! My friends and I think Football Player is sooo cute! Dad says Football Player is a man of integrity; he wants me to marry a guy like him. I can't believe doctors told his mom she should consider Abortion! I'm sure glad she didn't listen to them."

"Many people are thankful she chose Life! There is also Musician, whose then-teenage mother was the victim of rape. She was told by many that Abortion would be an okay choice because she became pregnant as a result of something awful being done to her. But she correctly believed that God had a destiny for her son, and she too chose Life. He and his band are now impacting many through the messages they communicate. I could go on and on, telling you stories of women who were told Abortion was an okay alternative, but because they chose Life, we have been blessed by the talents and abilities of their children."

"That's pretty amazing, Mom. I sure have a lot to tell Loyal, Patience, and Compassion when I see them again. My best friends have got to hear about all this. Thanks again for talking with me."

"I enjoyed it—even if parts of the conversation were tough to talk about, it was all necessary. And right now, young lady, it's time for you to get ready for bed."

"Awww Mom! Can't we talk just a few more minutes?"

"Not tonight—you've got school tomorrow! You know we can talk anytime."

"Okay ... good night!" Purity said as she kissed her mom and headed back into the house.

Wisdom stayed out on the porch a few minutes longer, quietly thanking God for the gift of a daughter who was eager to listen and apply counsel from her parents.

A Tish of Truth

One night God appeared to King Solomon in a dream and said: *What do you want? Ask, and I will give it to you!* Solomon could have requested anything in the world, but he asked God for an understanding heart—in other words, he asked for wisdom. God granted Solomon's request and also blessed Solomon with so much wealth that he could buy whatever he wanted.

Even with all his riches and possessions, Solomon said this about wisdom: *For wisdom is far more valuable than rubies. Nothing you desire can compare with it.* Ask God every day for wisdom. That is a prayer He is certain to answer. You'll be amazed at what God will do in and through you when you listen and choose wisely.

Hey again—it's Purity! Thanks for joining me on this exciting adventure. You've already met Wisdom, my amazing mom. She has some more important thoughts to share with you, so be sure and pay attention to her advice. Trust me … she knows what she is talking about. When I follow what she says, my life seems to go a lot better than when I do what I think is best. Listen closely … you'll be glad you did!

♥ Purity
XOXO

♥♥♥
Words of Wisdom

Hi Friend!

Purity and I are so excited you chose to be part of this adventure. We hope you enjoyed listening in on our conversation.

Were you surprised to hear about the enormous influence of Media and Entertainment in our culture? It's so important for you to understand the many ways messages are being communicated to you. Then you can make wise decisions about what you will and will not watch, read, and listen to. Simply changing the television channel or turning off an inappropriate movie can spare your mind and heart from being exposed to unnecessary and potentially harmful messages.

Maybe what you read in this adventure hit home because you just found out that you're pregnant. If that's you, please tell a trusted authority figure very soon. You do not need to keep this to yourself. If you're not sure who to talk to, ask God and He will show you. I believe you are going to make the *life-giving* decision God created you for. It may not be an easy road, but you will avoid much pain and heartache while getting to experience the many blessings that come from choosing Life.

If you are one who has gone through the pain of Abortion, please know that you are not alone. The enemy wants to tempt you to believe that you're the only one who feels guilt, shame, and deep waves of sadness that may catch you by surprise.

But I have good news for you! God already knows about the decision you made—and He still loves you unconditionally! He is simply waiting on you to call out to Him and receive forgiveness so you can get on the road to healing.

Please don't let this secret rob you any longer. God has a mighty plan for you, but staying silent will keep you locked in an emotional prison. Jesus is the key to freedom; He died on the cross so you could be set free. When you speak up by talking with someone you trust, you'll be amazed as the chains that have held you captive begin to loosen. Breaking the silence is a very courageous choice.

Have you ever received Jesus Christ as your Lord and Savior? I am not referring to simply knowing *about* Jesus from stories you've heard. But do you actually have a relationship *with* Him? When you receive the free gift of Grace through Jesus Christ, the Spirit of God comes to live within you and is always available to give you power to live victoriously and make wise decisions!

If you desire forgiveness and a fresh start, both are available to you today. Jesus gave His life for you so that the enemy can no longer take advantage of you and hinder you from living your destiny!

Purity and I are so proud of you!

Wisdom

A Prayer to Receive Grace

Dear Jesus, I have been trying to live in my own strength for too long. I know that I cannot be victorious in this life by relying on my own abilities. Today I receive the free gift of Grace that comes through You alone. I acknowledge that I am a sinner and I receive You, Jesus, as my Savior—the payment for my sins. Thank You that Grace cleanses me once and for all. Though I may still make mistakes, I do not have to live under condemnation because You have already forgiven me. Today I receive Grace and Your Spirit's wisdom and power that equip me to live victoriously. Thank You for these amazing gifts!

Thoughts for Reflection & Discussion

1) In what ways are you influenced by Media and Entertainment every day?

2) Do you feel pressure to look or dress a certain way because of what you see on television or in magazines?

3) What messages are being communicated through the television shows you watch and the music you listen to? Be specific; when you really start paying attention to the lyrics, you might be surprised what you've been listening to!

4) Wisdom used a big word—Desensitization—to describe the way Media and Entertainment can cause us to gradually accept words, actions, and ideas that we know are not right. How have you seen this happen in your own life?

5) Do your friends or other students at your school talk about Abortion?

6) It's obvious what Wisdom and Purity believe about Abortion, but what about you? Do think Abortion is a good or bad choice? How come?

7) What are some consequences of Abortion that Media and Entertainment don't usually tell you?

8) Describe the differences between Abortion and Adoption. For example, Abortion involves rejection of life while Adoption involves acceptance of life. Abortion results in death while Adoption results in life. Now it's your turn. What are some other differences?

Purity's Plan of Action

♥ In light of what you now know about Media and Entertainment, your challenge is to pay close attention to the songs on your iPod or phone. Do the lyrics contain profanity, sexual references, or are they in any way degrading to women? If so, how about deleting them from your music library. You can replace them with songs from artists who communicate positive messages—such as these beautiful and talented women:

o Britt Nicole

o Natalie Grant

o Francesca Battistelli

o JJ Heller

♥ Wisdom talked with Purity about being a life-giver. Some practical ways that you can give Life are through a hug, an encouraging card, or taking time to listen to someone who needs a safe person to talk to. Make a list of several people who you think could use a touch of Life. Then write down specific ideas of how you plan to give Life to them this week.

♥ If you are pregnant, scared, and unsure of what to do next ... or if you have experienced Abortion and are now battling guilt, shame, and regret, please talk with a trusted authority figure. That could be your parents, an older relative, youth pastor, or school counselor. Remember, silence keeps you trapped; it's time to for you to be set free!

Purity Meets Emotion

♥♥♥

"Guard your heart above all else,
for it determines the course of your life."

~ King Solomon ~

"May I go out for a walk around the neighborhood?" Purity asked as she came into the kitchen.

"That's fine," said Wisdom, Purity's mother. "Just make sure you're home by dinner—we're having your favorite meal!"

"Yes Ma'am. See you in a little while!"

Purity bolted out the back door, down the driveway, and onto the sidewalk. Being outside was one of Purity's favorite ways to relax. The exercise did her body good, and she could often think more clearly when out in nature.

Just a short ways down the sidewalk, Purity was startled from her thoughts by a voice behind her. "Excuse me, would you mind if I joined you on your walk?"

Purity turned and saw a girl who appeared to be her same age and surprisingly looked a lot like her as well. "Sure," responded Purity. "What is your name anyway?"

"My name is Emotion," said the girl, as she came alongside Purity. "I actually know you quite well, but I'm excited for you to finally become more aware of me."

"Well it's nice to meet you, Emotion," said Purity. "So ... what exactly do you want to talk about?"

"You're going to have to pay close attention, because this can get a little confusing," Emotion replied.

"Okay—I'm all ears!" replied Purity.

"Even though it feels like you are meeting me for the first time, the truth is that I have been with you since you were born." Emotion paused, watching Purity's reaction. "But now that you're getting older, I think it's the right time for me to tell you more about myself."

"Alright … I guess," Purity said a bit hesitantly. She didn't see any reason not to trust Emotion, who was certainly nice and friendly—and Purity couldn't help but notice again how much Emotion looked like her. "Go ahead and tell me whatever it is you think I need to know about you."

"Sweet! I was hoping that's what you would say!" exclaimed Emotion. "After you better understand me, hopefully you'll then know how to let me express myself in ways that are good and balanced. You know Purity, I'm a very real part of you—there's no denying that. And while it's okay for me to express myself at the right time, you must be careful not to let me—Emotion—control your life."

"Control my life? How or why would I let you do that?" asked Purity.

"That's easy," responded Emotion. "When you allow me to express myself in extreme ways, I will often end up influencing your beliefs and eventually your behavior."

Emotion waited for a moment, giving Purity time to think about what she had said. Then she continued: "I have a habit of making sudden and sometimes drastic changes depending on your circumstances. It's best for you to find the healthy balance of expressing me, while not letting me get the best of you. The more you are aware of me, the easier that will become."

"Wow—that was a mouthful," chimed in Purity. "So why are you just now introducing yourself to me, even though you said you have known me from the moment I was born?"

"That's an excellent question," Emotion replied. "I usually wait to introduce myself to girls until they are around your age because now is the time that you are developing into a young woman. That means there are changes going on in your body …"

"Okay, enough already! I know all about that," interrupted Purity. "My mom has already had this talk with me."

"Great! Then perhaps you also know that as your body is growing and changing, you will likely notice your expressions of me—Emotion—going up and down as well. That is why I said you have to learn to balance the way you handle me."

"I think I understand, but please keep explaining," encouraged Purity.

"Well … it may sound crazy for me to say—almost like I'm telling on myself, but sometimes you can't trust me," Emotion confessed. "My very reason for being in your life is to respond either positively or negatively to what's happening to you and around you. But my expression—which is the way you feel—may or may not be an accurate sign of what's really going on."

"So basically you're saying that if I'm not careful, what I am feeling can cause me to believe things that aren't even true."

"You got it!" Emotion replied.

"Could you give me some specific examples?" asked Purity.

In the midst of their conversation, the girls had stopped walking and were now sitting under a tree, facing each other.

"Sure I can," said Emotion. "Let's say you wanted to be included in a certain group of friends at school. But those girls made it clear to you that you were not welcome to join them. So this might be how you would see me express myself."

Purity watched as Emotion dramatically jumped to her feet. Then Emotion's expression suddenly changed. Her shoulders slumped over, her head hung low, and the look on her face was as though her favorite pet had just died. Emotion took a few steps forward, walking slowly and shuffling her feet. Just as quickly, Emotion's facial expression went back to normal. "Did you get that?" she asked with a grin.

"Oh my goodness—I can totally relate!" exclaimed Purity. "I met Rejection in the school cafeteria last week. I tried to go sit down next to her, but as soon as I put my lunch on the table, she got up and walked away. I was totally embarrassed and sad too, but I tried not to show it."

"Yep, I remember that day," Emotion stated. "And unfortunately you let me get the best of you that time."

"What do you mean?" Purity asked, somewhat confused.

"Well," began Emotion as she took a seat again on the grass next to Purity, "you were so focused on Rejection that you didn't even notice when Acceptance and Encouragement sat down next to you. They tried to talk with you, but you couldn't seem to forget how Rejection had tempted you to feel."

Purity thought for a moment. "So because I let you overreact to what happened with Rejection, it caused me to miss out on meeting new friends, right?"

"You got it again!" replied Emotion.

"I really do have to learn how to get you under control."

"It's more just that you need to find the balance. I am not always expressed negatively," continued Emotion. "Think of all the times when something super exciting happens. How do you respond then?"

Purity stared wide-eyed as Emotion hopped to her feet, turned several cartwheels, then started jumping up and down, whooping and hollering.

Almost as if reading Purity's mind, Emotion said, "Yea, I am kind of dramatic, aren't I?"

Both girls fell into the grass laughing hysterically. "Wow, you are funny," said Purity.

"Well, that may have been an exaggeration, but I was just trying to show you how quickly your moods can swing from one extreme to the other, simply by a change in circumstances."

"I think I get your point," Purity responded.

"How about another example?" began Emotion, as Purity braced herself for what might be coming next. "Let's say you are walking down the hallway at school, when Mr. Gorgeous looks your way and winks at you." Purity couldn't help but giggle as Emotion's cheeks turned a bright shade of pink, her eyelashes began to flutter, and she started to sway ... lost in the moment.

"Yes indeed, something like that would make me quite giddy!" Purity responded.

"Now what about this: My dad's name is Protection, and my mom's name is Wisdom. I love them both so much. My mom and I talk about everything, but there are times when she and I don't agree ... like about certain friends I want to hang out with, clothes I'd like to wear, and places I wish she would let me go."

Before Purity could even finish, she noticed Emotion once again change from being giddy, to suddenly looking quite angry. Emotion folded her arms across her chest. Her face was drawn in and tight, her lower lip stuck out in a pout, and her eyes squinted.

"It's amazing how fast you go from one emotion to the complete opposite!" Purity exclaimed. "I guess that means I am able to do the same thing, huh?"

"Absolutely; as a general rule, you can keep the following in mind," Emotion explained. "When something happens that you think is negative, if you are not aware of me, there is a good chance that I will tempt you to feel overly sad, depressed, or angry ... depending on the situation."

"That's pretty powerful advice," said Purity. "I can think of lots of girls my age who need to hear what you are saying."

"The important thing to remember is that you must stand on what you know to be the truth," Emotion continued. "Things that happen in your life may cause you to experience highs and lows with me. But as I told you earlier, I cannot always be trusted—especially with the negative situations. I tend to make them seem bigger and a lot worse than they really are."

"Like when I met Rejection at lunch," interjected Purity.

"Yes, that's right. You definitely need to give me the chance to express myself, since stuffing me is not healthy either. Sooner or later I will come out! So if you are sad and need to cry, then by all means cry! Just do not allow my expression to cause you to doubt what you know to be true, or change behaviors you know to be right."

"Wow, that is a lot to take in," said Purity. "But I can certainly see the importance of what you are saying."

"Do you have time for one more example?" asked Emotion. "It's a doozy!"

"Sure," responded Purity. "This ought to be interesting!"

"Awesome! Okay, think of those mornings when you wake up and start getting ready for school, but your hair just won't cooperate, your teeth suddenly seem yellow and crooked, there's a big zit on your chin, and you don't think any of your clothes look good on you. What happens?"

Once again, Purity watched in amazement as Emotion's facial expressions immediately changed. Emotion grabbed her hair with both hands and began wailing: "I'm sooooo ugly! I hate my hair! There's a boulder growing on my chin. None of my clothes fit! I am NEVER going back to school!!!"

"Oh my goodness!!!" Purity exclaimed, while attempting to stifle laughter. "I definitely have those kinds of days when it seems like nothing is going well. So your point is that if I allow you to run wild, I can overreact about a lot of things that happen in my life—things that really shouldn't be that big a deal. Is that right?"

"You got it," answered Emotion, nodding her head.

"Cool! Thanks so much, Emotion! I do want to give you the chance to come out when necessary, without letting you drastically affect my outlook on life. Would you like to come home and meet my parents?" Purity asked.

"That's okay," said Emotion. "Your mother and I have already met. I can guarantee you that she'll be glad to know we've spent some time talking. She will definitely be amazed when she sees you applying the principles we have discussed today!"

"I'll be sure to tell her about our chat. I better head home now," Purity said, as she stood and began walking the direction of her house. "I hope to see you again soon!"

Purity had already taken off down the sidewalk, so she didn't hear Emotion mutter under her breath, "Probably sooner than you think!" Then Emotion did a few more cartwheels in the grass ... just because she could.

A Tish of Truth

The extraordinarily wise and wealthy King Solomon once gave this caution: *Guard your heart above all else, for it determines the course of your life.* We are urged to protect or keep a close eye on what and who we allow to have access to our heart. Why? Because it is the foundation or source of all our emotions. If you and I allow our emotions to control us, our actions will likely follow whatever we are feeling at any given moment. This is important to remember because our actions will always result in either positive or negative consequences. Choose to act on truth and facts, not ever-changing feelings.

Hey again—it's Purity! Thanks for joining me on this exciting adventure. My amazing mom, Wisdom, has some important thoughts to share with you. Be sure and pay attention to her advice. Trust me ... she knows what she is talking about. When I follow what she says, my life seems to go a lot better than when I do what I think is best. Listen closely ... you'll be glad you did!

♥ Purity
XOXO

♥♥♥
Words of Wisdom

Hi Friend!

Purity and I are so excited you chose to be a part of this adventure. We sure hope you enjoyed yourself and discovered something new as you listened in on Purity's conversation with Emotion.

While God uniquely designed women with the tendency to be emotional beings, there still must be a delicate balance between expressing our feelings in a healthy way versus allowing our feelings to control us. Emotions that are properly communicated can positively impact the lives of those who cross our path. On the other hand, emotions that are incorrectly expressed or kept buried in our hearts can be quite destructive—both to us and to others. Because you are a one-of-a-kind young woman, circumstances will affect your heart differently than perhaps the effect that same situation would have on someone else.

Throughout your teenage years, it may take extra support to help you navigate the variety of feelings you are likely to experience. As your body is going through various hormonal changes, your emotions might fluctuate at shocking extremes! At times you may feel like you're riding an emotional roller coaster ... happy one moment, then plummeting into sadness the next—perhaps for no apparent reason! Someone who is several steps further down the road of womanhood—such as your mother or a mentor—can walk with you through this process.

Friend, if after reading this you've come to realize you are feeling some strong negative emotions, please seek out help from a trusted authority figure. If you are experiencing intense depression, insecurity, or feelings of rejection and have considered harming yourself or another person, you must tell someone as soon as possible. In most situations, your parents should be the first ones you confide in. However, if there is abuse going on inside your home, you might want to share your struggles with a trusted older relative like a grandparent, aunt, or uncle. Other possibilities could include a youth leader, teacher, school counselor, or coach. Whatever the case, do not keep unhealthy thoughts and emotions bottled up inside of you. There is absolutely no shame in asking for help; actually, Purity and I consider you to be extremely wise and courageous! Though sharing your true feelings may feel a bit scary and risky, it could actually save your life.

While the conversation between Purity and Emotion has given you some powerful insights, you are going to need supernatural wisdom to live victoriously in this area. James 1:5 says: *If you need wisdom, ask our generous God and he will give it to you.* That is an incredible promise! Sometimes wisdom comes in the form of a person who offers you counsel and advice. Other times wisdom is received through a thought or an impression in your spirit. It is vital that every source of wisdom always lines up with the Bible, which is the standard for Truth. And remember, if you are truly seeking wisdom, you will be watching for however God chooses to deliver it.

The ability to continually receive wisdom from God starts by first being in a relationship with Him. Purity and I believe this is the most important relationship you will ever have! It comes by recognizing your need for a Savior, then receiving the gift of salvation through Jesus Christ, God's Son. Jesus loves you so much that He gave His life for you by dying on a cross for all the times you would ever sin or make a mistake. Jesus took the punishment that you deserved, and He was victorious over sin and death by coming back to life three days after He died!

Jesus now lives in heaven with His Father, so God sent His Spirit to be with us here on earth. When you receive the free gift of salvation, the Spirit of God comes to live within you and becomes your source of wisdom and power to live victoriously!

If you have never before received Jesus Christ as your Savior, you can do so today. Remember, you are beginning an exciting new relationship with the God Who loves you unconditionally. When you receive His gift, you will then have access to supernatural wisdom that is needed to effectively apply the advice Purity and Emotion shared with you!

We are so proud of you!

Wisdom

A Prayer to Receive Grace

Dear Jesus, I know that I cannot be victorious in this life by relying on my own abilities. Today I receive the free gift of Grace that comes through You alone. I acknowledge that I am a sinner and I receive You, Jesus, as my Savior—the payment for my sins. Thank You that Grace cleanses me once and for all. Though I may still make mistakes, I do not have to live under condemnation because You have already forgiven me. Today I receive Your Spirit's wisdom, power, and gifts that equip me to live victoriously. Thank You!

Thoughts for Reflection & Discussion

1) What did you think about Emotion? In what ways does she remind you of yourself?

2) It's funny to see Emotion come to life in this way, because she so appropriately represents us as females. Unless we choose to bring our emotions into balance, they can rule our lives. What specific emotions come to mind that you need to do better at handling (Examples: Anger, Jealousy, Sadness, Insecurity)?

3) Have you ever met Rejection? How did you respond to him or her?

4) Were you able to identify with the sudden changes of Emotion? How so?

5) What are some dangers in allowing our emotions (or feelings) to direct our decisions and outlook on life?

6) Sometimes when people have experienced deep hurts in life, they will "stuff" their emotions in an attempt to not feel any more pain. While they may think this protects them, what else does shutting off their emotions do?

7) At this point in your life, what person generates the strongest emotional reaction from you (Examples: Mom, Dad, a friend, that guy you think is sooo cute!)?

8) Perhaps the most important statement Emotion makes is the following: *Things that happen in your life may cause you to experience highs and lows with me. But as I told you*

earlier, I cannot always be trusted—especially with the negative situations. I tend to make them seem bigger and a lot worse than they really are. You definitely need to give me the chance to express myself, since stuffing me is not healthy either. Sooner or later I will come out! So if you are sad and need to cry, then by all means cry! Just do not allow my expression to cause you to doubt what you know to be true, or change behaviors you know to be right.

o   What is the main point you take from Emotion's advice?

9) Describe a time when you allowed your emotions to convince you that something negative was true ... then you later found out what you had believed was totally wrong.

Purity's Plan of Action

♥ This may be a bit humbling for you, but it will be worth it! Find a trusted authority figure in your life—whether that be your mother, grandmother, aunt, sister, or an older friend. Ask them the following questions about yourself:

o Do I allow my emotions to control my actions? If so, how?

o In what areas am I entirely too emotional?

o Are there any places where it seems I tend to shut off my emotions?

♥ For the next week, pay extra close attention to yourself throughout the day. Make a note of how you respond when scenarios similar to the following take place. It may give you a good idea as to how much of an emotional response you have to circumstances in life:

o **Your best friend hangs out with a new student more than you at school one day.** Do you become jealous, hurt, angry, and ignore her ... or are you happy that she has another friend too?

o **You wake up and start getting ready for school, only to realize three massive pimples have formed on your face overnight.** Do you scream and tell your mother you refuse to go to school for the next week? Or do you ask your mom or older sister for some make-up to cover up the bumps and try to make the best of the situation?

o **You find out a group of classmates have been saying untrue things about you when you are not around. Their words really hurt your feelings.** Do you spout off angry words back at them? Do you stuff the pain and act like it doesn't bother you? Do you confront them about what they've been saying? Or do you simply choose to ignore them?

o **You are grounded for the weekend because you chose not to clean your room after having three days to do so.** Do you yell at your parents, *Life's not fair* ... then slam your bedroom door, and pout the rest of the evening (By the way, I really hope you are not allowed to get away with that kind of behavior—it is quite disrespectful!)? Or do you take responsibility for your actions by apologizing and immediately going to clean your room?

o **You have noticed a really good looking guy a couple grades older than you. After finding out he now has a girlfriend,** do you lock yourself in a bathroom stall and cry uncontrollably, believing that your hopes for a date to the senior prom (which is still several years away!!) have been dashed? Or is it no big deal, since after all there are plenty more guys should you ever be interested?

Purity Faces Body Image

♥♥♥

"Laughter can conceal a heavy heart, but when the laughter ends, the grief remains."

~ King Solomon ~

It was overcast and chilly outside … perfect weather for an afternoon inside at the mall. Purity and her best friends—Loyal, Patience, and Compassion—were going to eat lunch and then do some shopping. Purity's mother—Wisdom, as well as Compassion's mother—Discernment, had brought the talkative, giggly girls to the food court at the mall.

"I'm starving!" Patience exclaimed. "Me too!" the other three girls chimed in.

"What are you all in the mood for?" asked Discernment.

"Pizza!" "Tacos!" "Smoothies!" the girls replied.

"Well, it sounds like everyone wants something different, so how about you each go get your food while we wait here."

Wisdom and Discernment smiled as the girls took off. Purity was the first to return.

"Mom, there are several girls from school sitting at that table. Do you mind if we go eat with them?"

"That's fine. We'll sit a couple tables away."

Purity waited for her friends; then they walked over to the table. One of the girls looked up and smiled.

"Hi, Purity! Are you all coming to eat with us?"

"We sure are—if you don't mind."

"We'd love for you to join us!"

"Thanks! Let's introduce each other since I don't know your friends, and you don't know mine," said Purity.

"Sure thing; my name is Mia, and this is Ana."

"I'm Moshi," piped in another girl.

Purity introduced her friends as they sat down and began eating. "Have you all been here long?" asked Patience.

"No, our moms dropped us off a little while ago," answered Moshi. "Ana's mom, Denial, is still here. She's at a table close by."

As Compassion bit into her taco, she noticed that Ana was the only one at the table who wasn't eating—yet she was intently eyeing the other girls' food. Compassion thought Ana's eyes looked really sad and tired ... and she seemed thin compared to the other girls at the table.

"What are you girls up to after you eat?" asked Purity.

"We're going to a movie," responded Moshi. "It's called *Thin is In* ..."

"... and I am sooooo excited to see it," interrupted Ana. "Some of my favorite celebrities—like Supermodel, Movie Star, and Pop Singer—are in the movie. Those ladies are gorgeous, and their bodies are totally perfect. I can't wait to find out their secrets!"

"How do you know so much about those celebrities?" asked Loyal.

"I spend lots of time watching Pop Singer's music videos on YouTube ... but the way I find out the juicy details of their lives is when I go to the grocery store with my mom ..."

"Seriously? At the grocery store?" interrupted Loyal.

"Of course! While my mom is waiting in the checkout line, I look through the latest issues of Fashion Fads and Trendy Teens. Sometimes I even slip one into the cart when my mom's not paying attention. That way I can read it cover-to-cover when I get home. Those magazines are filled with pictures of Supermodel, Movie Star, and Pop Singer. They give me great tips for what my body should like, what's cool to wear, and how to get a guy's attention."

"So ... do you think there's a chance that those pictures are influencing you to try and stay skinny ... because that's what they want you to think being beautiful is?" Patience cautiously asked, then continued.

"It seems like Supermodel, Movie Star, and Pop Singer often go to extreme measures to keep what they would consider to be a perfect body. Plus, I've heard that those magazine pictures are airbrushed—which means they fix the pictures to make them look perfect."

Patience's thoughts went unanswered because Mia crumpled up her sandwich wrapper, stood up, and excused herself. "I'll be right back," she said, while quickly walking away from the table of girls.

"There she goes again," Ana said quietly.

"What do you mean?" asked Purity.

"She always goes to the bathroom after she eats."

"How come ... is she sick?" Loyal asked. She and the other girls looked rather confused.

"You could say that. Her name—Mia—is short for Bulimia."

"I've heard that word before, but I'm not sure what it means," said Compassion.

"Bulimia is a type of eating disorder where a person eats a lot of food in a short time period—that's called binging," explained Ana. "Then they feel guilty and purge, which means they get rid of the food they just ate."

"Oh how awful!" responded Compassion. "Does Mia know she has a problem?"

"She knows her actions aren't normal, but I don't think she'd call it a 'problem'. This has been going on since Mia was in third grade—that's a long time. From what Mia has told me, sometimes when people have this habit, they prefer to eat alone so no one sees how much they are really eating. But Mia only cares when a teacher or other adult is watching; then she tries to hide it. Otherwise she just eats and then goes straight to the bathroom."

"Do you know why Mia does this?" asked Loyal.

"Not really. I asked her one time but she said she didn't want to talk about it. The only other thing she said is that this works for her right now, and since it's not hurting anybody, it's not a big deal."

"Well it's got to be hurting Mia!" exclaimed Purity. "Does she not realize that?"

"If so she doesn't seem to care," responded Ana.

"Ana … I couldn't help but notice that you're the only one who isn't eating anything," said Compassion. "Were you not hungry?"

"Oh no, I'm not hungry. I ate half of a banana for breakfast, so that will hold me over until dinner. Then I'll eat a couple bites of whatever my mom cooks."

Purity and her friends all looked at each other, clearly shocked by what Ana had said.

"Are you serious, Ana? That's all you're going to eat today?" asked Patience.

"Well yeah, that's normal for me. My body is used to it, so I'm rarely hungry anymore."

"I don't get it," said Loyal. "What's so bad about food that you don't want to eat?"

"If I eat too much, I won't be able to look like Supermodel and Pop Singer. The articles I've read about them say they often go on crazy diets and exercise for a long time each day. I figure

74

if it works for them, I should do it too. I mean, look at how many people just love them!"

"What I don't understand is why you think you have to look like Movie Star and other famous women? Why can't you just be happy with you?" asked Compassion.

"Because the way I am now is not good enough …"

"Now that's a lie, Ana!" interrupted Purity. "God made you beautiful—inside and out! He has given you lots of talents, and I know so many people at school who love you!"

"That's nice of you to say, but clearly you don't see what I see when I look in the mirror. Plus, my dad and mom never pay attention to me. I mean, if I need clothes or something they'll buy it for me, but they don't ever just sit and talk to me."

"I'm so sorry," Compassion said, her face showing the sadness she felt for Ana. "So what does your mom say about your eating habits? Has she even noticed?"

"Well, I play with my food a lot—you know … use my fork to move food around on my plate. Every once in a while I'll take a small bite. I know my mom is watching me but she has never said anything about my eating. So all I can figure is that she either doesn't want to believe I have a problem, or she just doesn't care enough to talk about it with me."

"I'm sure your mother cares about you," said Loyal.

Ana looked in the direction of the restrooms, where Mia had disappeared to.

"One time Mia offered me a laxative. I think she felt sorry for me because she noticed I rarely eat. She told me she had the perfect solution ... where I could eat all that I wanted to, without having to worry about gaining weight. But the thought of using a laxative, and then having to hang out near the bathroom until it kicked in, didn't seem like a good idea to me."

"Me either," chimed in Patience. "That sounds awful."

"Yea, I told her no thanks and that I'd just stick to not eating. So then Mia said she had another idea that I might like better."

"What was it?" asked the still wide-eyed Patience.

"Apparently when Mia doesn't use laxatives, she just forces herself to throw up. That sounds like an even worse idea, but she says you get used to it after a while."

"I don't mean this ugly," spoke up Loyal, "but I noticed Mia's breath smells really bad. Does that have anything to do with her purging as you called it?"

"It must. I can't give you all the scientific reasons, but every time Mia talks to me, her breath smells the same way. The last time she went to have her teeth cleaned the dentist told her the enamel on the backside of her teeth is coming off. Apparently he talked all hush-hush to Mia's mom after the appointment. On their drive home, her mom asked if she was making herself throw up because the dentist said tooth decay can be a sign of Bulimia. Mia lied and told her no; her mom hasn't brought it up again."

About that time Mia walked back towards the table. Her mouth was smiling, but Compassion thought Mia's eyes looked very sad. "Is everything okay, Mia?" she asked.

"Of course it is. What did I miss while I was gone?"

"Well," began Ana, we were just talking about food. "You'd think it would be an easy topic, but it's become quite difficult."

"How so?" asked Mia.

"Well, my friends and I all enjoy eating … probably too much!" Purity said with a grin. "But for Ana, food seems to be a big problem."

"Food is certainly not a problem for me!" Mia exclaimed. "In fact, I believe food is the friend that will always be there for me—it's totally true. If I'm sad, food cheers me up. When I'm angry, food calms me down. Food celebrates with me when something good happens. And if I'm lonely, food keeps me company so I don't feel so alone."

"I totally agree with Mia," piped up Moshi, who had been quiet until now.

"So Moshi," began Purity, "is your name short for something, like Ana and Mia's names are?"

"Yea, it is. Moshi is short for Emotional Eater. I eat when I'm happy, sad, bored, excited, angry, or lonely—you name it, I can find a reason to eat!"

"You do sound like you have a lot in common with Mia."

"Yes and no," responded Moshi. "Mia eats a lot of food in a short period of time, then feels guilty and purges it by using laxatives or making herself throw up. I don't purge; I just enjoy my food and let it comfort, support, encourage … whatever I need at the time."

"Does your mom know that's how you feel about food?" asked Loyal.

"If so she hasn't talked with me about it. I've definitely gained some weight from eating so much. My mom had to take me to get some new jeans the other day since all mine were too tight. But maybe she just thinks the extra weight is because I'm a teenager now. It may sound strange to you girls, but being a little fluffy, as I like to call it, actually helps me feel more safe … especially around older men."

"Really … why?" asked Compassion.

"I don't think older guys and men will look twice at a girl who's not skinny and perfect like Ana. I used to be really skinny and cute, but then … well … let's just say something happened that made me realize it's safer to be fluffy."

Compassion was intently watching Moshi's eyes. They looked increasingly sad the more she talked. Perhaps that was why she had been silently listening to the other girls.

"So do you believe food is the friend that will always be there for you—as Mia believes?" asked Patience.

"Absolutely. So far food has never let me down."

"That's interesting," responded Loyal. "So food is like an enemy to Ana, but it's a friend to you and Mia. Just out of curiosity, how long do those positive feelings from food last?"

"Uh ... well ... no one's ever asked me that before, so I guess I've never really thought about it. Seeing as how I have to keep eating in order to not feel so sad or lonely, maybe that means food isn't helping me as much as I thought it was."

The look on Moshi's face showed that a light bulb had turned on in her mind.

"So what happens if you're angry about something, but there isn't any food around? What do you do then?" asked Patience.

"Now that's just a nightmare ... especially if I'm with other people. I have to try and stay calm, take deep breaths, and not think about food. But the more I try not to think about it, the more food haunts me and becomes all I can think about! It's very frustrating. But as soon as I can find food to eat, I feel so much better."

"It kind of sounds like you may be addicted to food."

"Call it what you want," Mia flippantly replied, clearly coming to Moshi's defense. "But we've gotta have food to stay alive you know."

"That's true, but I remember hearing someone once ask: *Do you eat to live, or do you live to eat?*" Purity let the question linger a moment before she continued. "In other words, food does have some very important purposes in that it gives us nutrition and energy—and most people enjoy eating with friends and family. But there may be a problem if food is our focus from the time we wake up until we go back to sleep."

"Well so far food has helped me get through middle school, so I don't see a need to change anything," said Mia.

"I agree!" Moshi added.

As the girls ate the last bites of their lunches, a woman approached the table.

"Hi Mom," said Ana. "Purity, you and your friends haven't met my mom yet. Her name is Denial."

"It's nice to meet you," the girls all said.

"Same to you," responded Denial. "Ana, are you girls finished eating? The movie starts in ten minutes!"

"Oh that's right! We were so busy talking, I almost forgot about going to see *Thin is In*." Compassion noticed Moshi's eyes look down. In light of everything Moshi had just shared, Compassion thought it strange that she would want to watch *Thin is In*. Her countenance showed she wasn't really looking forward to it.

"We hope you have fun!" said Purity, as Mia, Moshi, and Ana gathered their things and stood to go. "Thanks for letting us sit with you. Maybe we can talk some more soon."

"That sounds good," responded Ana. "We'll see you all at school on Monday."

Purity and her friends threw their trash away, and then headed to the table where Wisdom and Discernment were sitting.

"So how was your lunch?" asked Wisdom.

"The food was great," said Patience. "But the talk we had with the girls was kind of sad and shocking."

"How so?"

"Well ... we just got into an unexpected conversation about food—it was pretty eye-opening to hear some of the things Ana, Mia, and Moshi said. Basically Ana starves herself, Mia eats a lot and then gets rid of it by making herself throw up or by using laxatives, and Moshi eats pretty much all the time—food is her best friend."

"Wow! You girls did get an earful then," said Wisdom. "Would you like to know some possible reasons why many people struggle with food-related issues?"

"Yes, please" answered Compassion. "I'm having a hard time understanding why those three amazing girls would treat their bodies so poorly."

"The absolute most important thing I could tell you," began Wisdom, "is that Anorexia, Bulimia, and Emotional Eating are not so much *food* issues as they are *heart* issues."

"Now that's definitely not what I was expecting you to say, Mom," Purity stated.

"But it's the truth," continued Wisdom. "So for those of us who don't have those same struggles, we can actually cause more problems if our only goal is to treat the symptoms of under-eating or overeating."

"Do you mean by forcing Ana to eat, and by keeping food away from Mia and Moshi?" asked Loyal.

"That's exactly right," Wisdom responded. "Requiring someone to change their actions, without even addressing their heart, could result in much anger, frustration, and further pain for them."

"Why?" asked Patience.

"Because their actions are merely symptoms of a deeper heart issue; if the heart is not being lovingly pursued, the symptom may go away, but the root problem hasn't been dealt with. So the issue will likely resurface, or simply change to another imbalanced behavior."

"Okay ... that makes sense," said Loyal. All the girls watched Wisdom closely as she continued.

"There are always exceptions ... like if a girl has been starving herself, and her health and life are at risk, then of course the symptoms would need to be addressed immediately. But it can't stop there; as her physical health is stabilizing, her heart—or emotional health—will also need to be lovingly dealt with."

"I'm so glad you told us that," replied Compassion, "because I really wanted to go buy Ana some lunch and nicely ask her to please eat it. She looked so hungry, even though she said she wasn't."

"That shows your sympathetic heart, but unfortunately it's not usually that simple. This may surprise you girls, but both Anorexia and Bulimia could actually be considered slow forms of suicide."

"What?!?!" exclaimed Purity, clearly shocked at what Wisdom had said. "I thought suicide was when someone killed themself ..."

"Think about it," chimed in Discernment. "God gave us food to fuel our bodies; without food people become malnourished and will eventually die."

"That's true, so ..." said Compassion.

"So when a young woman will not allow herself to eat, quite literally she is slowly killing herself through starvation. But the same is true for the opposite extreme ... someone struggling with Bulimia may take in a lot of food, but then they quickly purge it out so the nutrients don't have a chance to be absorbed by their bodies."

"Mom, we have got to do something! We can't let Ana and Mia keep on doing this to themselves!"

"I know, Purity, and I am so thankful you girls have sensitive hearts that care about Ana, Mia, and Moshi. Perhaps I should talk with Ana's mom."

"Her mom's name is Denial—we just met her. She brought the girls to the mall and is taking them to see *Thin is In*." Purity could not help but notice the look that passed between her mom and Discernment.

"Let me guess," began Discernment. "Denial acts like she doesn't know Ana has a problem ... right?"

"How did you know that?" asked Loyal.

"This may be a bit difficult to understand, but as mothers, even though we want what's best for our children, there are times when we may fear looking like a bad parent if we admit our child really has a problem. I can't say that's definitely what's going on with Denial, but if she were to acknowledge that Ana has a problem, then she might think it reflects poorly on her as a mother—as if she is the reason Ana is struggling."

"I get that," said Loyal, "but it would seem like Ana's health and life should be far more important than Denial's fear of possibly looking like a bad mother. I mean, she'll look like an even worse mom if something awful happens to Ana."

"You are a very wise young woman," Discernment said.

"Ana told us she has to be thin because of the way Supermodel and Pop Singer look," Patience spoke up.

"And while that may be what she truly believes, behind that reason there are likely insecurities that result in her having a distorted body image."

"Oh ... so that's why Ana said: *You don't see what I see when I look in the mirror* when I tried to tell her she is beautiful," Purity interjected. "But she also told us that her parents never pay attention to her."

"Exactly," continued Wisdom. "And there you have the root of her problem! It sounds like she feels unloved and like she doesn't matter, so she is looking elsewhere—my guess is Fashion Fads and Trendy Teens—to see what Supermodel, Movie Star, and Pop Singer are doing to get noticed."

"Wait a second," piped in Loyal. "How did you know Ana looks at Fashion Fads and Trendy Teens? We didn't even tell you that!"

"Those two magazines are extremely popular today. Many teenage girls read them without realizing they are being programmed to dress, act, and look a certain way," answered Wisdom. "That's why I tell Purity to look the other direction when she is with me in a checkout line. It doesn't matter if you are a young girl, teenager, or adult woman ... just a quick glance at the front cover of Fashion Fads tempts you to feel bad about your body because none of us can possibly be as perfect as an airbrushed Supermodel."

"Wow!" said Patience. "I'm going to look the other way the next time I am waiting in line at the grocery store. Thanks for that advice."

"Ana's heart is hurting because she doesn't have the attention of her parents—the most important people in her life. So the *symptom* of starving herself is actually a cry for attention. That's certainly not always the root of an eating disorder, but it seems to be the case for Ana."

"Mom, didn't you say there are other reasons for having a poor body image that can lead to an eating disorder?" asked Purity.

"Yes … there are countless triggers—control is another big one. Let's say a teenage girl was in a situation as a young, innocent child where she was taken advantage of and felt completely out of control … like being sexually or physically abused. That can cause her to feel quite vulnerable."

"What does vulnerable mean?" asked Compassion.

"It means she feels unsafe, like she is exposed with no one to protect her from harm. So she might then grasp for any area in which she can gain some sort of control … such as how little or how much food she eats."

"I don't get it. Not eating, or eating too much, harms her body even more."

"Yes, it does, but there is also another thing to consider in abuse-type situations. That's the element of shame. Oftentimes when a little girl is taken advantage of, she will then go on to feel guilt and shame—believing she did something to cause the abuse. That couldn't be further from the truth, but it's a familiar line of thinking with abuse victims. They start to believe it was their fault, so then something like not eating— or over-eating and forcing themselves to throw up—becomes a form of self-punishment."

"Oh goodness ... I am so sad for Ana and Mia," said Compassion.

"Me too," added Patience. "Do you remember what Moshi told us ... that being 'fluffy' helped her feel safe around men? She also said something happened that made her realize this ..."

"That is exactly what Wisdom was referring to," said Discernment. "Again, we don't know the full story, but based on what Moshi told you girls, it sounds like she intentionally keeps some extra weight in hopes that she won't catch the attention of men. You girls are right—that is very sad, as she has likely been hurt by a man who took advantage of her."

"I wish there was something we could do," said Loyal.

"Well you girls know that you can always pray for Ana, Mia, and Moshi. God knows their hearts—He sees the pain there, and He wants them to be healed even more than you girls do," Discernment explained.

"We'll definitely pray for them," said Purity.

"Other than praying, you can continue being friends with them. Clearly they all desperately need to feel unconditionally loved and accepted. Ultimately that kind of love comes through a relationship with Jesus, but you girls have an important opportunity to demonstrate His love every time you see them. You may be amazed at what happens. I have a feeling your conversation impacted them far more than any of you realize right now. Wisdom and I are so proud of each of you."

"There's a lot more that could be said about this," said Wisdom, "but why don't we go shop for a while. We can talk more later on."

"That sounds good to us!" said the girls, as they gathered their belongings and headed towards the mall area.

A Tish of Truth

King Solomon had so much money he could buy whatever he wanted ... but no possession or person could bring him lasting happiness. He once said: *Laughter can conceal a heavy heart, but when the laughter ends, the grief remains.* You live in a culture that encourages big smiles, lots of make-up, flashy accessories, and fashionable clothes—in an attempt to paint an external picture that everything is okay ... even if your heart is hurting. But just as Solomon said, when the laughter ends ... when the make-up is washed off, the accessories are removed, and the lights are turned out at night, your grief remains.

So where do you turn for comfort? Is it food, friends, clothes, or entertainment? While these options may provide a temporary reprieve to cover up your pain, only a relationship with Jesus Christ offers lasting comfort and healing for your heart.

Hey again—it's Purity! Thanks for joining me on this exciting adventure. You've already met Wisdom, my amazing mom. She has some more important thoughts to share with you, so be sure and pay attention to her advice. Trust me ... she knows what she is talking about. When I follow what she says, my life seems to go a lot better than when I do what I think is best. Listen closely ... you'll be glad you did!

♥ Purity
XOXO

♥♥♥
Words of Wisdom

Hi Friend!

Purity and I are so excited you chose to be part of this adventure. We hope the lunch conversation you listened in on opened your eyes to what has become an epidemic in our culture—that of heart pain and unhealthy body images which can often lead to eating disorders.

This topic is especially close to my heart because I struggled with it for eight long years. The battle was so intense it left me contemplating suicide; I could not see a way out of this horrible trap.

I realize now that from a very young age I had a tendency to look to food—especially sugary sweets—for comfort. God certainly gave us food as a gift to enjoy and to provide our bodies with necessary nutrients. But my desire for certain types of food was imbalanced and extreme.

When I was 17 years old, the distorted body image I'd developed over the years began to be expressed through an addiction to running and strictly limiting my food intake. This lasted for one-and-a-half years and resulted in numerous health issues. Then an emotional trigger caused a shift to the opposite extreme, and for the next six-and-a-half years I secretly binged on enormous amounts of unhealthy food—all while being an external picture of health and fitness. I felt like such a hypocrite, and was haunted by guilt and shame.

It isn't necessary to share specific details of the roots or causes of my struggles with food. What's most important for you to know is that it all stemmed from my heart being in a lot of pain—perhaps you can relate.

For years I buried my pain by spending every waking moment practicing and playing the game of basketball. I appeared to be very successful ... my team won lots of games; I received many awards, and earned much recognition—including a full scholarship to play basketball at a well-known university. But the ache and sadness in my heart remained, no matter how many points I scored.

Friend ... what are you using to bury your pain? Can you relate with me, Ana, Mia, or Moshi? Far too many girls and guys your age are fighting this battle. If it's not a struggle for you personally, more-than-likely a friend or someone you know is trapped in an eating disorder.

I spent years trying to "get over" this through my own determination and willpower. I hated my inability to stop the binges. The shame and guilt I felt was almost unbearable. Several key things happened that led to this struggle being overcome.

First, I came to the end of myself. I finally realized and admitted that what I was doing was never going to work. All my best efforts at getting better resulted in setbacks and repeats of the binge-guilt-shame cycle. When I reached this point of desperation, God introduced me to an incredible woman who quickly became my spiritual mother. She taught me some key truths that are so powerful I want to share them with you.

Though I had memorized Bible verses from the time I was a little girl, I was confused as to why I was not living a life of power and victory. My spiritual mother was the first person to ever tell me the truth that there is a *thief* (Satan) whose main *purpose is to steal and kill and destroy.* She helped me understand that this struggle was actually the plan of an evil enemy who wanted me dead, and was doing everything possible to keep me stuck in this awful cycle.

Most important, my spiritual mother introduced me to the true nature of God—His unconditional love, empowering grace, and infinite wisdom ... as well as the gifts of His Spirit that equip us to live victoriously. My whole life I had believed God to be distant, disinterested, and demanding—a harsh judge who closely watched me just to see what I did wrong, so He could then punish me.

My life was forever changed when I grasped the reality that Jesus Christ died to give me abundant life so that I didn't have to be trapped by the enemy any longer. I stopped *trying to get better* and simply *received His grace* that transformed my heart and empowered me to walk in victory!

After eight long, dark years of struggle, the healing of my heart miraculously came about in just a matter of days and weeks. *The root was a heart issue, so when that was resolved, there was no more food issue!*

What about you? Have you ever met this Jesus Who saved, healed, and delivered me? Not just in knowing *about* Jesus from stories you've heard, but do you actually have a relationship *with* Him? When you receive the free gift of Grace through Jesus Christ, the Spirit of God comes to live within you, and is always available to give you power to live victoriously!

If this relationship is something you desire, you can receive it today. Jesus gave His life for you so that the enemy can no longer take advantage of you and hinder you from living your destiny!

Purity and I are so proud of you!

Wisdom

P.S.—I am not a professional or medical expert, so please do not take my advice as the final word. As I told Purity and her friends, if you have been struggling with an unhealthy body image or an eating disorder, please talk to a trusted authority figure immediately. Your health and ultimately your life could be at risk. Know that it can't stop there; as your physical health is stabilizing, your heart—or emotional health—will also need to be lovingly dealt with. God wants you to be fully healed and whole!

A Prayer to Receive Grace

Dear Jesus, I have been trying to live in my own strength for too long. I know that I cannot be victorious in this life by relying on my own abilities. Today I receive the free gift of Grace that comes through You alone. I acknowledge that I am a sinner and I receive You, Jesus, as my Savior—the payment for my sins. Thank You that Grace cleanses me once and for all. Though I may still make mistakes, I do not have to live under condemnation because You have already forgiven me. Today I receive Grace and Your Spirit's wisdom and power that equip me to live victoriously. Thank You for these amazing gifts!

Thoughts for Reflection & Discussion

1) How does what you see in magazines, movies, and television shows affect how you feel about your looks and overall appearance?

2) The Bible has a pretty amazing passage related to body image. It's found in Psalm 139:13-14 and says: *You made all the delicate, inner parts of my body and knit me together in my mother's womb. Thank you for making me so wonderfully complex! Your workmanship is marvelous—how well I know it.* Is it difficult for you to believe that God made you *wonderfully complex* and *marvelous*?

3) Why do you think it's so hard for most of us to truly appreciate our uniqueness instead of wishing we looked like other people?

4) If you could change one thing about your appearance, what would it be (Examples: to be shorter or taller, to have a smaller nose...)? Why do you want this part of you to be different?

5) Eating disorders are widespread in today's culture among girls and boys, women and men—no age or gender is immune from this dangerous and potentially life-threatening trap. After reading about Ana, Mia, and Moshi, did you see your actions and views of food as being similar to:

   o   Ana—starving yourself in hopes of being thin?

   o   Mia—binging and purging?

o   Moshi—eating all the time because food is your best friend?

6) Do you agree with Wisdom and Discernment's thought that *food issues* are usually caused by *heart issues*? Why or why not?

7) What have you used to bury or cover up pain in your heart (Examples: food, friends, sports, hobbies, or entertainment)?

Purity's Plan of Action

♥ There are some practical steps you can take to guard your eyes, mind, and heart from the over-exposure to airbrushed, unrealistic images that shape your body image. Consider the following ideas:

o Do as Purity does when waiting in a check-out line— look the other way instead of glancing at the front covers of magazines. One look is all it takes to get your mind thinking about all the ways you *don't* look like those touched-up images.

o The Internet is a constant bombardment of women with seemingly perfect figures. Be aware that every time you click on a new page, you are likely going to see advertisements with images designed to program your mind into believing the way those women look is normal. What websites should no longer be on your list of favorites?

o While you cannot avoid every airbrushed picture, you can certainly control what you choose to look at. Are there certain magazines you need to get rid of and not purchase again? What about television shows you no longer need to watch? You will be amazed how much easier it is to maintain God's perspective (*wonderfully made* and *marvelous*) when you are not filling your mind with what the world says you need to look like.

♥ While check-out lines and bookstores have countless options of appearance-focused magazines, there are some excellent alternatives available that speak a different and powerful message. Listed below are some highly relevant and informative, picture-filled magabooks you can find in the *Teen* section of the *Store* at www.VickiCourtney.com. These are Purity's favorites:

o *TeenVirtue: Real Issues, Real Life... A Teen Girl's Survival Guide*

o *TeenVirtue 2: A Teen Girl's Survival Guide to Relationships*

o *TeenVirtue Confidential: Your Questions Answered about God, Guys, and Getting Older*

♥ If you, or someone you know, are struggling with an eating disorder, please talk with a trusted authority figure about it as soon as possible. Feel free to show them this story if you need help explaining the thoughts you are experiencing about yourself, your body, and/or food. I am proud of you!

Purity's Road Trip with Protection

♥♥♥

"Listen to your father, who gave you life …"

~ King Solomon ~

The colorful leaves, bright blue skies, and cool air were evidence that the fall season had settled in for a few weeks before winter arrived. This was Purity's favorite time of year. Both Purity and her father, Protection, loved being out in nature. A few days earlier Protection had asked Purity if she would like to take a drive in the mountains with him, to look at all the fall colors, and spend some time talking. Purity readily agreed, and was super excited to hang out with her dad for the day.

When Saturday morning came, Purity and Protection quickly got ready, grabbed their jackets and the snacks Wisdom—Purity's mother—had packed for them; then they headed towards the mountains. The one-on-one times spent with her dad were some of Purity's best memories. She felt incredibly special and safe when she was with him. Some girls might say Protection spoiled Purity, but she believed he simply treated her the way all dads should treat their daughters—like they were the most treasured girl in the world!

Moments into the drive, Purity began to chit-chat, hardly pausing to take a breath. "Alright, Dad, I'm guessing you planned this trip to talk to me about guys. Is that correct?"

"Maybe so," Protection responded, with a twinkle in his eyes.

"Well, that's cool and all. Since that's the subject of the day, I have a really important question for you … If you could design the kind of man you want me to marry, what would he be like? I want to hear all about him!"

"Wow—that is a great question!" said Protection. "I'm so glad you asked."

Purity turned to face her dad, anxiously awaiting his response.

"Well," said Protection, grinning as he spoke, "I believe the man who would make a perfect husband for you is named Valor!"

"Uh ... seriously? Who in the world is Valor?" exclaimed Purity, clearly confused. "I've never heard of such a man!"

"Calm down! That's what I'm about to explain to you," said Protection, amused at Purity's dramatic reaction.

"For starters, Valor is a man of courage and strength. He is known for his exceptional bravery during times of danger ... like in battle. Because Valor doesn't show fear, the enemy will never know if he is afraid."

Purity's expression made it clear that she didn't understand where in the world Protection was headed with this. "Dad, why are you talking about going to battle and being brave? Do you think I'm going to marry a man in the army or something?"

"Actually, yes ... I do! But probably not the kind of army you're thinking of," responded Protection.

"Okay then, I need more explanation please."

"Listen closely because this is very important," began Protection. "I want you to marry a man like Valor because God created men to not only be the physical protectors of their wife and family, but the spiritual protectors as well."

"It sure sounds like men have a lot of responsibility," said Purity, clearly interested in what her father was saying.

"They sure do ... and God uniquely designed them to be able to handle it as they rely on Him to help them. There may be times when your husband needs to guard you and your family from potential dangers, but every single day he will have opportunities to go to war on your behalf in the spiritual realm."

Protection paused a moment, then continued. "Far too many men don't realize that there is a very real and active enemy who is seeking to destroy marriages and families. That enemy is Satan, and he will use whatever means necessary to wound members of the family, turn them against each other, and ultimately tear them apart. If there is a husband and father in the home, it is primarily his duty to keep watch, making sure there aren't any open doors for the enemy to have access into his household."

"Wow, Dad. That sounds pretty important. Are you a man of valor for Mom and me?" asked Purity.

"I sure hope to be," responded Protection. "I'm certainly not perfect, but God's grace gives me the wisdom and strength that I need."

"I think you're pretty amazing!" said Purity. "Oh ... and what exactly is an open door?"

"An open door is a way that the enemy can gain entrance into your life and home. The television would be a prime example."

"How so?" asked Purity.

"If the man of the house allows certain shows to be watched in his home—like horror and occult-based programs or movies, that provides an open door for a spirit of fear to come right in and take up residence in the home. So his children might begin to experience nightmares until that fear is dealt with."

"Oh my goodness!" Purity exclaimed. "I know many girls at school who watch movies and read books about vampires. They think it's totally harmless, yet several of them have mentioned the awful nightmares they can't seem to get rid of. I am so thankful you are telling me this, Dad. It's starting to make more sense why you and Mom won't allow me to watch those kinds of movies, or read certain books and magazines."

"Without a doubt," began Protection, "everything you watch or look at will affect you sooner or later in some way. Once you see those images, they will always be imprinted in your mind—and may resurface at the strangest times."

"Well those girls have to know they are putting themselves in danger. I need to tell them to be careful!"

"I'm glad you are so concerned about their well-being," Protection responded. "But you've got to keep in mind that so many dark, occult-related objects and experiences—like vampires, magic, and horoscopes—have been mass-marketed in a way that presents them as harmless and fun. Girls your age might not understand that playing with a Ouija board at a slumber party can open a door to evil that negatively affects them for years." Protection paused, allowing his words to sink in. "The world of darkness is nothing to mess around with or treat as a game. And while all that is true, you need to be cautious and gracious when talking with your friends about this."

"I'm just kind of shocked right now," said Purity. "I've heard girls at school mention all the things you referred to. I know that they aren't good for us, but why exactly?"

"The simplest reason I can give you is from Ephesians 5, which tells us to *live as people of light!* It goes on to say: *Take no part in the worthless deeds of darkness; instead, expose them.* The Bible is also clear that *God is Light, and there is no darkness in Him at all.* So as children of God, we are not to engage in activities that are evil, dark, and potentially quite dangerous."

"Well that seems easy enough to understand ... but lots of people aren't listening to those instructions. I've heard the guys in my grade talk about their video games—some sound really freaky, with lots of blood, killing, and other stuff that sounds too evil to be called a game."

"But Purity, even with all that's been said, I cannot stress to you enough that we do not focus on the enemy or his works of darkness. I am simply informing you of the reality of open doors so you can be wise in what you choose to look at, listen to, and expose yourself to in any way. Ultimately we know that Jesus' death and resurrection brought victory over evil and darkness. Our focus is Jesus and His finished work on the cross!"

"I totally get that. Dad ... do you really think I'll be able to find Valor—a man who knows and lives all these important things you're sharing with me?" asked Purity. "I mean, this is deep stuff! Not many people talk about it."

"God will absolutely bring you a man with these values! Jesus said, *Keep on asking, and you will receive what you ask for.* And God promises to give you the desires of your heart, so just ask Him to bring Valor to you at the right time. Then you patiently wait until He does—which is sometimes easier said than done!"

"Thanks for the reminder. I know you are my amazing earthly dad, but God is my heavenly Father Who loves to give me good gifts, right?" ask Purity.

"You got it!" replied Protection. "Your mother and I love nothing more than to surprise you with gifts ... but God has infinite resources and knows exactly what will be best for you!

"Now let's go back to the open door conversation for a minute. I'll give you one more example. When the man of the house is secretly viewing pornography on the Internet, he has allowed perversion to enter his home. So he shouldn't be surprised when his son or daughter also develops a fascination with pornographic material."

"I never thought about that before, but it makes sense. So what is the best way to close doors, or to keep the family safe—in the spiritual realm?" inquired Purity.

"That's another great question! First and foremost, the man of the house needs to be in a growing relationship with God," Protection said, before continuing. "That does not mean following a long list of 'dos and don'ts.' Rather, he simply needs to receive God's grace, power, and wisdom that are freely available so he can become all that God designed and equipped him to be for his family. That is the foundation which everything flows out of."

"So if we stay focused on God's grace," began Purity, "and make good decisions using the wisdom He gives us, open doors won't even be an issue."

"Yes, you are exactly right! Grace is what gives us power to overcome. Like I told you before, we don't ever give too much credit to the enemy. However, the Bible does make it very clear that we are to *stay alert* because we have an enemy who *prowls around like a roaring lion, looking for someone to devour.* One way he devours is by sneaking into peoples' lives through an open door they were clueless about. He doesn't play fair, that's for sure! But what's really amazing is that God is a Restorer …"

"What's a Restorer?" Purity interrupted.

"Well, God loves to give back or *restore* all that the enemy has stolen from us. Each of us have made costly decisions or experienced painful circumstances. But God takes our mess and redeems it—meaning He can bring good out of what looks like nothing but bad. Then He restores by giving back far more than we ever lost!"

"WOW!! That's awesome ... and it gives us hope! I sure do appreciate you taking time to hang out with me and talk about these things. Even though it's not normal talk for girls my age—and lots of kids at school would think it's weird—I still know it's important."

"Purity, you are an extremely wise young woman to even be listening and taking these truths to heart. I couldn't be more proud of you!"

"Thanks, Dad."

"Something your mother and I do occasionally is pray through or *cleanse* our home."

"Now what in the world do you mean by that?" asked Purity.

"We go from room to room, telling anything evil or impure to leave in the name of Jesus; it is not welcome in our home. This is especially important when moving into a new place, because only God knows what all has happened on that property. So we want to cleanse the land and home, and dedicate it to Him."

"That sounds pretty intense," Purity commented.

"Most important, we ask for the peace and special presence of the Holy Spirit to remain in our home. Many people have commented on the peaceful feeling they experience when they come visit."

Protection paused a moment before continuing. "There have been many times that your mother and I have come into your room at night and prayed over you while you were sleeping. Prayer, truth from God's Word, and the discernment of the Holy Spirit are vital to continually walk in spiritual victory."

"That is so cool, Dad; I didn't know you and Mom do all those things! Thanks for the many ways you keep me safe. I sure hope my friends' parents do the same for them!"

"So to sum all that up," began Protection, "while I do want you to marry a man who is strong, brave, and capable of protecting you from physical danger, the first priority is a husband who understands his role as Valor—the spiritual protector of the home. As you begin to be attracted to the guys around you, you'll be able to tell which one is Valor as you observe their character. Your mother and I will also help you with this."

"I never imagined that this would be the first answer you'd give me! But it was a good one; I sure have lots to think about. So other than Valor, what are some more qualities you think I should look for in guys ... and eventually my husband?" asked Purity.

"Hold that thought for just a moment," said Protection. "I'm going to pull off the road so we can find a big rock to sit on and continue talking. Have you been noticing the view all around us?"

"I sure have, Dad. It's so pretty! I just love the mountains and the different colored leaves. Thanks for bringing me up here."

Purity and Protection put their jackets on and headed over to the nearest smooth rock.

Protection continued the conversation: "Probably the best way to describe the type of guy I hope you marry would be to compare the many different kinds of men who are out there."

"That sounds interesting," said Purity. "Go ahead."

"Okay, the first men to compare are Pride and Humility. Pride thinks very highly of himself. He has an air about him that says to everyone around him, *I believe I am better than you.* Pride may think he is the best-looking, most talented athlete, and most popular guy in school. But people are not usually drawn to Pride ..."

"I totally know who Pride is," interrupted Purity. "He's the best player on the high school soccer team ... and he is not afraid to let everyone know it! But nobody likes to hear him talk about how many goals he scored in the most recent game."

"There is a big difference between Pride and Humility," Protection continued. "Humility is always looking for ways to put others first. He doesn't need to be the center of attention; in fact, he would rather let others be in the spotlight. Humility is content to serve without being noticed—yet he still has a strength that is quite attractive."

"Ohhhh ... he sounds like a great guy!!" Purity thoughtfully said. "I would love to meet him!"

"And by the way, Pride and Confidence are also two very different kinds of men. Women are drawn to Confidence because he is a leader who steps up and does whatever is needed, yet he doesn't brag about himself to others. So which do you think has the better character?" asked Protection.

"Most definitely Humility ... and Confidence too," answered Purity.

"You are exactly right; now on to compare Lust and Love. These two really are complete opposites. Lust is totally selfish; he is always looking to have his own wants and desires met. Love, on the other hand, is selfless. He is far more concerned with how he can help meet your needs and desires."

"Lust sounds awful—I don't understand why any girl would fall for him."

"Oftentimes Lust is able to attract young women who are desperate for attention from their father," responded Protection. "When Lust comes along and appears to be interested in them, that's when they fall for him."

"And I bet he ends up hurting them ... right?" asked Purity.

"Yes, unfortunately that is often what happens. Lust constantly pursues your treasure. Notice I did not say he pursues your heart—this is extremely important, Purity. Lust is only after your body. You better run fast from Lust if he ever tries to approach you."

"I will, Dad. And I'm going to warn my friends about Lust too."

"Love is completely different from Lust. Love will do whatever it takes to protect your treasure, save it for marriage, and then keep it safe within marriage. Love pursues your heart, not your body."

"Wow!" exclaimed Purity. "I'm going to start asking God to introduce me to Love. It would be so amazing to marry a man like him!"

"Yes—he would make a great husband for you," Protection agreed. "Similar to Lust, you might also come across Flattery. He will try to make you feel special with charming words that express his approval of you. But really, Flattery's motives toward you are selfish. Like Lust, Flattery wants to use you to get something for himself."

"I don't want anything to do with Flattery or Lust," said Purity.

"Sincerity is a much different man than Flattery or Lust. You'll know Sincerity by the way his actions back up his words. He won't say nice things to you and then expect you to give him something in return. Sincerity's compliments of you will likely be followed by actions that are in *your* best interest first and foremost."

"He sure seems like a nice guy," added Purity.

"Sooner or later you will probably encounter Dishonor and Respect," continued Protection. "You might hear about them before you even meet them, because they have very distinct reputations. Dishonor is unfortunately known for being dishonest. He may have a habit of cheating on tests, lying to his teachers and classmates, and speaking disrespectfully to those in authority over him. So whenever Dishonor does get a girlfriend, he will no doubt handle her in the same way. Dishonor doesn't treat anyone very well."

"I'm not interested in meeting him," said Purity. "How about Respect ... what's he like?"

"Respect is the opposite of Dishonor! People admire Respect, and have a very high opinion of him. Respect values everyone he comes in contact with, no matter what color they are, how much money they have, or what kind of car they drive. He is held in high esteem by all who know him, and even those that don't know him personally have heard of his good reputation. One way you'll be able to tell if you've met Dishonor or Respect is by listening to how he talks about his mother and sisters."

Purity thought for a moment. "I've not yet met him, but I am pretty sure Respect is in the eleventh grade. Lots of the older girls talk about him, and say what a great guy he is."

"If you are willing to wait and not lower your standards or settle for any guy that shows interest in you, God will certainly bring His best choice into your life at just the right time," Protection encouraged. "You may meet him during high school, college, or it may be years later. But I want you to always remember that while you are waiting, both you and your future husband are being prepared for each other. God is growing your character and faith, and is doing so much

work in each of you. When the time is right for the two of
you to begin your lives together, then God will orchestrate
circumstances to allow you to meet."

"I know you are right, Dad, and I do want to wait for God's
best. I've already seen too many girls at school be so desperate
for a boyfriend that they will do anything a guy asks. The
sad part is that those kinds of guys usually end up dumping
the girls shortly after they get whatever it was they wanted.
Then the girl gets sad and depressed. I don't want to make
the same mistake."

"Of course there are many more guys you'll meet over the
next few years," said Protection. "I've shared some of the
main ones with you today. My prayer for you is not just that
you meet Humility or Respect. I am praying that the husband
God has hand-picked for you will be all those qualities
combined and more!"

"I'm going to ask God for that too," Purity declared.

"I guess Love would be the man I most want you to marry,
because Love is humble, respectful, sincere, and above all else,
unselfish. Love will lead and protect you; Love is a man of
valor—courageous and ready to go to war on your behalf, yet
he has a kind and sensitive side as well. Because God is Love,
I believe He wants you to experience Love as a husband."

"This is almost too much to take in! I cannot wait to tell my
friends. They need to know what kind of men to look for ...
and what kind to stay away from! Thanks, Dad, for sharing
all this with me!"

As Protection and Purity walked back to the car, Protection silently thanked God for giving him a daughter who was wise enough to listen to her father's counsel. Many girls Purity's age thought their parents were old and out-of-touch. Purity was not that way, and it had already kept her out of a lot of trouble.

Protection rolled down the windows and opened the sunroof. He and Purity spent the rest of the afternoon admiring the scenery and enjoying each other's company. More than once throughout the drive, Purity thought how blessed she was to have such an incredible dad—one who loved her enough to spend time talking with her about the important things in life. Purity reached over and grabbed Protection's hand, then smiled as she felt him give her hand a squeeze that said *I love you.*

A Tish of Truth

It's sometimes easy to think your parents or other authority figures don't have a clue what they are talking about. Yet King Solomon—a man of extreme wealth and influence—once said: *Listen to your father, who gave you life.* Much heartache can be avoided and many blessings will be received if you are wise enough to listen to and act on advice given by those in authority over you.

Hey again—it's Purity! Thanks for joining me on this exciting adventure. My amazing mom, Wisdom, has some important thoughts to share with you—so be sure and pay attention to her advice. Trust me … she knows what she is talking about. When I follow what she says, my life seems to go a lot better than when I do what I think is best. Listen closely … you'll be glad you did!

♥ Purity
XOXO

♥♥♥
Words of Wisdom

Hi Friend!

Purity and I are so excited you chose to be a part of this adventure! We sure hope you enjoyed listening in on the conversation between Purity and her dad.

So ... what did you think of Protection? I can tell you from firsthand experience that he is an incredible husband and father! Being married to Protection has been one of the greatest gifts of my life! Our marriage has not been perfect— we've certainly encountered some bumps along the way. But having a husband who is the leader of our home has provided much security and peace. Protection looks to God to supply him with the wisdom he needs to effectively love and take care of mine and Purity's hearts. My husband truly is a man of valor—humble yet courageous, and a mighty warrior in the spiritual realm. Purity has told me several times that she wants to marry a man just like her father—now that's an incredible compliment!

I realize that it may have been difficult for you to listen in on Purity's conversation with Protection. Perhaps you don't have a father in your life at all, or maybe your relationship with your father is far different than what you saw between Purity and Protection. If this is true of you, I am so sorry for any hurts and pain in your heart.

In so many ways, our earthly fathers paint a picture in our minds and hearts of what we come to believe God is like. For example, if your dad divorced your mom and makes little effort to see you, then you might be tempted to think that God will also abandon you. Or maybe you have a father in your home, but the only time he interacts with you is when he yells at you for doing something wrong. This might tempt you to believe God is a mean judge who is constantly looking for reasons to point a condemning finger at you.

My friend, nothing could be further from the truth. Even the best of human fathers make mistakes and fall far short of showing what God, our heavenly Father, is really like. In Hebrews 13:5, God promises that He *will never fail you* or *abandon you*. You can be confident that, no matter what you have experienced from your earthly dad, your heavenly Father will absolutely *never* leave you. He loves you unconditionally—so much so that He sent His Son Jesus to die on a cross to pay for all the times you would ever sin or make a mistake. Now that's an incredibly loving Father!

Because Jesus now lives in heaven, God sent His Spirit to be our Comforter and Guide while we are here on earth. When you receive the free gift of salvation, the Spirit of God comes to live within you and becomes your source of wisdom and power.

If you have never before received Jesus Christ as your Savior, you can do so today! There is no need to be nervous. Talking to God is no different than talking to your friend. Remember, you are beginning an exciting new relationship with the heavenly Father Who created you and has a mighty purpose for your life!

Purity and I are so proud of you!

Wisdom

♥♥♥

A Prayer to Receive Grace

Dear Jesus, I know that I cannot be victorious in this life by relying on my own abilities. Today I receive the free gift of Grace that comes through You alone. I acknowledge that I am a sinner and I receive You, Jesus, as my Savior—the payment for my sins. Thank You that Grace cleanses me once and for all. While I may still make mistakes, I do not have to live under condemnation because You have already forgiven me. Today I also receive Your Spirit's wisdom, power, and gifts that equip me to live victoriously. Thank You for bridging the gap between me and God. I am excited to begin a relationship with my heavenly Father.

Thoughts for Reflection & Discussion

1) What did you like most about Purity's father?

2) Does Protection remind you at all of your father, or a father-figure in your life? How so?

3) In what ways is Protection different from your father or father-figure?

4) Protection told Purity he wanted her to marry a man like Valor. Have you ever met a guy who had qualities similar to Valor? If so, describe what he was like.

5) How do you feel when you are around Valor (Example: safe, loved, protected ...)? Be specific!

6) What do you think about Protection saying a husband is responsible for protecting his family both physically and spiritually? Perhaps you should ask your father if he does this!

7) Protection talked at length to Purity about *open doors* that can give the enemy (Satan) access into a family's home and lives. Which of the examples Protection gave have you been involved with?

8) List the television programs you watch most often, movies you've seen recently, and books or magazines you read. Could any of them could be an open door?

9) Protection compared several different types of guys. Go through the following list and write out the differences between:

   o   Pride, Confidence, & Humility

   o   Lust & Love

   o   Flattery & Sincerity

   o   Dishonor & Respect

10) From the above list, circle which ones you have met before. Then share how you felt around them (Example: *"I met Lust at a ball game; he was kind of creepy … I could tell he wanted something from me"*).

11) Of all the men Protection described for Purity, which one would you most like to marry? How come?

Purity's Plan of Action

♥ If you have a personal relationship with God through Jesus Christ, the Holy Spirit is the One Who leads you into all truth. Ask Him now to show you if there are any open doors in your life that need to be closed and removed (like throwing away certain books, dvds, etc). If the Holy Spirit reveals anything to you, talk with a parent or trusted adult and get their permission to trash the item(s) as soon as possible. If He shows you an open door that is not in your possession (such as a movie you saw last year or a game you played with friends), as well as for any items thrown away, pray the following prayer out loud to break off any harmful connections: *Father God, thank You that You are Love and You always have my best interest in mind. I recognize that (___fill in the blank___) was an open door for the enemy to have access into my life. I thank You that the blood of Jesus continually cleanses me and purifies me, and I ask Him to do that now. I repent of having opened that door, and right now I choose to close that door so that it no longer has a right to negatively affect me. I rely on the strength of Your power at work within me to help me never open that door again. Thank You for Your unconditional love and grace. Thank You that I am Your favored daughter. I receive all that You have for me!*

♥ Write out specific qualities for the type of man you want to marry. God created you, and knows the unique desires of your heart. Having them written out will help you not settle for less than God's best. It will also be a continual reminder of what you are asking God to give you in a husband. Share what you've written with a trusted friend or family member who can encourage you as you wait for the man you will one day marry.

Acknowledgments

Adventures with Purity wouldn't be a reality had it not been for the prayers, support, and insights offered by my younger sister, Jenni, and my spiritual mother, Laura. I am grateful for your willingness to share the wisdom you've acquired through years of experience in your roles as daughters, sisters, wives, mothers, mentors, teachers, and leaders. Thank you both for believing in me and the message God birthed in my heart to deliver!

A special thanks to my mother, Sherry, for encouraging me to read. In so doing, you gave me the opportunity to dream, imagine, learn, and be inspired. Thank you for wisely limiting my time in front of the television; though I may not have appreciated it then, I certainly do now!

Many thanks to my older sister Angie ... you are an incredible mother, teacher, and example for your children. You give sacrificially in countless ways; they are so blessed to call you *Mom.* I am proud of you—just because you're you.

All of us have individuals who impact our lives from a distance. I'm grateful for the ways in which each of these women has influenced me:

... Vicki Courtney and Dannah Gresh: Thank you for equipping women of all ages with valuable truth and insights. Only God knows the heartache that has been avoided because a young woman or mother heeded your counsel. You continue to bring life to many.

… Janet Parshall: Thank you for the high level of integrity you demonstrate as you help us navigate the bustling marketplace of ideas. You are a much-needed example of how to keep one foot firmly in the Word of God and the other in the daily headlines. Thank you for being an advocate for life, liberty, and truth.

… Former Alaska Governor, Sarah Palin; and Minnesota Congresswoman, Michele Bachmann: Thank you for being *life-givers* who boldly proclaim life in a culture that continues to devalue it. You are modern-day versions of biblical Esther: beautiful, courageous, and empowered by the Spirit of Almighty God to impact a nation. We are blessed to have your leadership.

… Pam Tebow: Thank you for choosing life.

Additional Resources

♥ For Tweens
   o Magabooks by Vicki Courtney
      • *Between: A Girl's Guide to Life*
      • *Between Us Girls: Fun Talk about Faith, Friends, & Family*
      • *Between God & Me: A Journey through Proverbs*

♥ For Teens
   o *Sisterhood Magazine* with Susie Shellenberger
   o Magabooks by Vicki Courtney
      • *TeenVirtue: Real Issues, Real Life ... A Teen Girl's Survival Guide*
      • *TeenVirtue 2: A Teen Girl's Survival Guide to Relationships*
      • *TeenVirtue Confidential: Your Questions Answered about God, Guys, and Getting Older*
   o *His Girl: A Bible Study for Teens* by Vicki Courtney
   o Books by Dannah Gresh
      • *What Are You Waiting for? The One Thing No One Ever Tells You about Sex*
      • *And the Bride Wore White: Seven Secrets to Sexual Purity*
      • *Secret Keeper: The Delicate Power of Modesty*

♥ For Moms
   o Books by Vicki Courtney
      • *5 Conversations You Must Have with Your Daughter*

- *Logged on and Tuned Out: A Non-Techie's Guide to Parenting a Tech-Savvy Generation*
- *Your Girl: A Bible Study for Mothers of Teens*

o Books by Dannah Gresh
  - *8 Great Dates for Moms & Daughters*
  - *6 Ways to Keep the "Little" in Your Girl: Guiding Your Daughter from Her Tweens to Her Teens*

References

Purity Discovers Peer Pressure

- ♥ Proverbs 13:20
- ♥ I Corinthians 10:13

Purity's Spa Night with Wisdom

- ♥ Proverbs 8:11
- ♥ Proverbs 4:23a
- ♥ I Peter 5:8-9a
- ♥ Revelation 12:9
- ♥ John 8:44
- ♥ I Kings 3:5

Purity Meets Emotion

- ♥ Proverbs 4:23
- ♥ James 1:5

Purity Faces Body Image

- ♥ Proverbs 14:13
- ♥ John 10:10
- ♥ Psalm 139:13-14

Purity's Road Trip with Protection

- ♥ Proverbs 23:22a
- ♥ Ephesians 5:8b,11
- ♥ I John 1:5b
- ♥ Matthew 7:7
- ♥ I Peter 5:8
- ♥ Hebrews 13:5

About the Author

Rebekah Joy is the founder of 333 Insights, which was established on the promise of Jeremiah 33:3 and exists to share wisdom that is enlightening, empowering, and enduring. Her life's passion is in knowing God and discovering the remarkable secrets He desires to communicate. She resides in southeast Tennessee and enjoys coming alongside others to develop challenging *iron sharpening iron* relationships.

Also by Rebekah Joy

7:21—A Gripping Account of Religious
Deception and Divine Pursuit

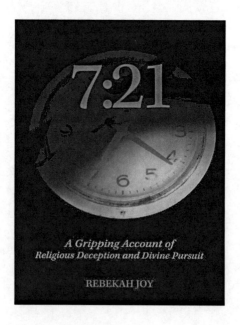

With billions of people on planet earth, have you ever wondered if God really notices you? And if He is indeed aware of you, is it possible that He would ever speak directly to you and your specific circumstances?

Perhaps your view of the divine is that of distant and demanding, a deity who places high expectations yet offers no help in meeting them. Maybe your spirit is hungry for authentic encounter with a source that can truly satisfy.

7:21 is the true and powerful story of divine pursuit through the unique avenue of meaningful spiritual dreams. For a woman caught up in the world of performance, striving, and the unspoken pressure of having to appear as though she always had it together, her way of life was suddenly interrupted by an intense, thought-provoking dream. When its meaning became clear, there could be no denying the invitation being lovingly and intentionally extended to her.

7:21 offers hope for the hopeless, rest for the weary, relationship for the religious, and astonishing revelation for those hearts who long to hear God speak.

CPSIA information can be obtained at www.ICGtesting.com
Printed in the USA
LVOW13s2150141013

356846LV00005B/47/P